A Cook's Tale

Centauri Survivors Second Chance Chronicles, Book Two

J. Alan Veerkamp

A NineStar Press Publication

Published by NineStar Press
P.O. Box 91792,
Albuquerque, New Mexico, 87199 USA.
www.ninestarpress.com

A Cook's Tale

Printed in the USA
First Edition
May, 2018

Print ISBN: 978-1-948608-72-5

Also available in eBook, ISBN: 978-1-948608-68-8

Warning: This book contains sexually explicit content, which may only be suitable for mature readers.

After a breakup, Erron Murfin finds himself broken, homeless, and destitute. The chance to become the Santa Claus's new cook is a beacon he can't ignore.

The new position allows him to work under Gamin Rockwell, the man who helped raise him until he disappeared when Erron turned nineteen—well over a decade ago. While the two make up for lost time, Erron catches the eyes of many crewmen as well as James and Barrus, a married pair with real intentions who are determined to draw the cautious new arrival into their relationship.

Even as he stitches together his ability to see a future for himself, Gamin's history and personal issues begin to surface. Secrets bubble out in ways Erron can't ignore and he finds himself with a mystery he needs to solve.

Because there's something about Gamin that goes far deeper than the fatherly role he once held in Erron's life so long ago.

Chapter One

"IS IT TRUE there aren't any heteros on board your ship?" Erron Murfin leaned forward in the darkened diner.

The ruggedly handsome man sitting across from Erron was softly lit by the amber glow emanating from the table's frosted acrylic surface. Dark stubble lined Erron's dining partner's jaw in perfect rhythm with the subtle, yet masculine facial lines that hinted at a man not afraid of an honest day's work. A touch of predator in the other man's blue eyes, the last bit of food passed his lips. The meal had been simple but well crafted. Erron couldn't recognize any synthesized food.

Being outside the main dinner hours, the diner was sparse with patrons. The walls were painted in dusky colors with a soft metallic luster. Soft murmurs of conversation were audible if one bothered to listen, but Erron tuned it out, focusing on the dirty-blond alpha male across from him. The examination from across the table was intense, but he wasn't unnerved by the attention. It only served to amplify his curiosity.

Captain Danverse swallowed and answered. "No hetero, no female. That's the rule."

Erron cocked his head. "No female, either? Aren't you afraid of being labeled a misogynist or tagged as a discriminatory employer?"

"I've been called that before." Danverse didn't seem the slightest bit ashamed of the fact. "When I set up my crew, I made the ship open to everyone at first, but we had problems. A female passenger walked in on a group of my boys fooling around in the shower. They said they didn't approach her and I believe them, but she felt threatened enough as the only woman on board to lodge a formal complaint that almost cost me my ship. A lot of my crew have nowhere else to go and we all nearly lost our homes. I had to make a hard choice and keep things simple. No gender issues. No orientation conflicts. I wanted to populate my ship with men who worked hard and enjoyed each other's company when the voyages were long. Same rules apply to the occasional passenger. It wasn't the most progressive decision I've ever made, or popular, but I believed it necessary at the time."

"And now?"

"Almost ten years later, I have my boy at my side, I have a life I love, and I work with my best friend and adopted family. I always believed that you don't fuck with it if it isn't broken. But I may be willing to rethink it down the line."

Danverse lifted his glass and took a solid sip of the dark whiskey. "But I'm not here to be interviewed for a job. You are." A soft, growling laugh rolled off the captain.

Erron worked to keep his smirk from flaring into a full grin. "You're right. Ask away. What would you like to know?"

"First off"—glass still in hand, Danverse pointed at Erron—"why is the no-hetero rule so important to you?"

The smirk flattened as memories raced to the surface. Erron ran a hand through his shock of jade-green hair and settled back into his chair. Studying the captain, he decided how forthcoming he was going to be. The pain was still there, fresh and raw, but there was little to be done about it.

"I could use a break from the majority these days." If he thought Danverse was paying close attention before, it now appeared his interest had quadrupled. The captain's scrutiny was palpable.

"Boyfriend dumped you?" Danverse seemed to notice the sudden flush in Erron's cheeks. Without responding, Erron knew he'd revealed the truth. "You didn't know he was bi?"

Erron glanced away into a dark corner. "Not until he announced his engagement to her."

"Ouch."

Erron shrugged in a feeble attempt to shed the past. There was still the sharp pinch of loss in his chest whenever he relived what happened. If he wanted this job, he knew he wouldn't be able to brush this off. However, facing Danverse while he told his tale wasn't an option. If there was pity in the captain's eyes, he didn't have to witness it.

"I worked with him at the restaurant his father owned. We kept things quiet. We didn't want the rest of the staff thinking I was getting preferential treatment. I thought everything was great until the announcement. When she found out about me, she insisted I be let go. Little overprivileged bitch."

"She must have been quite a prize."

Erron snorted. "Trophy is the word that comes to mind. Too pretty, too whiny, and seemed like the type who'd been told since she was a little girl how much better she was than everyone else. Toby's father arranged their meeting, and her family was obscenely wealthy. It was all a business deal for him. He sacked me in a heartbeat and didn't even flinch.

"To top things off, when she found out he owned the building I lived in, she had me evicted. I've been living off my savings since." Erron drew a long, slow inhale. It wasn't just being thrown away that pained him so badly. The whole experience had made him more bitter and worthless than he'd been in his entire life. Not having the slightest clue of what was happening behind his back left him feeling profoundly stupid. It was the sort of thing that happened to a wide-eyed teenager, not a man in his early thirties.

"When did this happen?"

He rolled his eyes upward as he counted backward on his mental calendar. "About three months ago."

"Where have you been living?" A scowl was forming on Danverse's face, and Erron shrank in his seat.

"In some of the shittiest inns the spaceport has to offer."

"No friends to stay with?"

Erron shook his head. "Apparently, they took Toby's side after the breakup. It must be much nicer to rub elbows with a wealthy socialite than an unemployed, homeless cook."

"What about family?"

"It was just me and my mom, but she didn't survive the Centauri Civil War." Erron shrugged. "That seems like a long time ago."

Unconsciously, Erron crossed his arms over his chest, but not for warmth. Danverse's visible displeasure increased as he heard more about Erron's state of affairs. The more he said, the worse the expression became, and Erron was convinced the job opportunity was fading faster and faster.

"So what made you apply for our cook's position?"

"Needed a job and came across the Subspace Link ad. I did a little research on the *Santa Claus*. It looked like a good fit for me, and when I found out Gamin was part of the crew, I had to take a shot."

Danverse's brow perked. "You know our head chef?"

"Yeah. He was my mom's best friend when I was a kid. I never knew my dad, and he was the next thing to a father back then. They had some major falling out back when I was nineteen, and he stopped coming around. Mom never said what. Then the civil war broke out, and in all the craziness, we lost touch. I didn't even know he was alive until I found your advert. I figured I needed a fresh start, and touching base with him was something I should have done ages ago."

Danverse's stare intensified as the pause extended into a long, uncomfortable moment. Erron fidgeted in his seat as he envisioned his employment hunt begin again.

"Assuming I take you on, the job is every day, three meals a day. You'll have downtime, but not days off, except when we're in port. Gamin would be your direct superior, but there is still a chain of command. Living on board isn't a pleasure cruise, but it's not a bad life. The crew is like a small town. We're in each other's business, and we always look out for each other. I don't have a tolerance for people who can't play well with others."

Erron's eyes widened. Why was he telling him this? Surely, the captain wasn't saying yes?

"It sounds perfect. I'm not afraid of hard work, and Gamin's the reason I became a cook in the first place. Cooking makes me happy. I'm still waiting for you to tell me the downside."

Danverse's frown shifted into a sly grin. "Right now, I don't think I'm seeing one."

"Are you saying I can have the job?" Erron's voice peaked as he fought to control the excitement rising in his chest. There was no doubt he wanted the job, but he didn't want it to be so horrifically obvious.

"Can you be at Landing Bay Gamma Seven One tomorrow by 09:00 hours? We'll be in port for about a week, but I can have my security chief get you settled in before we ship out."

The smile on Erron's face made his cheeks ache. He was so elated. If he wasn't careful, he was going to be on the verge of tears. "You're Goddamn right I can be there."

Danverse lifted his glass in salute. "Well then, Mr. Murfin. Welcome to the crew."

ERRON LOOKED DOWN at the synthesized protein masquerading as eggs on his plate. How this diner justified serving this travesty was beyond him. Even the smell was wrong. It was nothing like the meal he had eaten during his interview yesterday. He picked at the unyielding rubber surface with his utensil and promptly set it down on the table. There was no way he was eating this. The triangle of toast was passable. At least they had real bread. It wasn't helping to settle his stomach, though, because his nerves were so on edge.

This diner in the spaceport was close to the *Santa Claus*'s landing bay. It was really the only reason he had chosen it. It certainly wasn't for the four-star cuisine. At least from his seat, the anti-grav pallet was visible, holding the crates with all his worldly possessions. Erron had packed as soon as he'd returned to his room the day before. When he'd realized he couldn't sleep worth a damn, he had given up trying. Now he had time to burn before his appointment. He wasn't sure if showing up too early was good or not. He didn't want to seem *too* eager.

Captain Danverse had told him he'd meet with his security chief for his indoctrination. There was a ship tour, procedures to go over, and a work contract to sign. Two years off planet wasn't really so long. From what he'd researched, most crew members extended their contracts multiple times, so the *Santa Claus* couldn't be that bad. On the plus side, he'd be allowed to cook for others again. That might make up for most shortcomings. Erron was fairly confident he was doing the right thing. Fairly.

It wasn't as if he had much choice. He needed the job. When the server brought the bill for his breakfast—rather than call it a travesty—he cringed when he pressed his finger to the DNA ID scanner. If there hadn't been enough credits in his account, he would have been in trouble.

He didn't know why he continued to sip at the bitter, burned coffee. It certainly wasn't doing his stomach any favors. The diner was stocked with a fair number of customers. Apparently, being cheap overrode the food quality in this establishment. Erron mentally kicked himself. Being a food snob was one thing, but being an elitist ass was something else. These people probably hadn't spent three months living in shitty hotels.

The patrons seemed mostly working class, enjoying their breakfasts. No doubt some were station regulars, who chatted with the servers and cook with a family-like familiarity. A warm camaraderie filled the place and that made Erron smaller somehow. What he wouldn't give to belong somewhere. He'd lost that when Toby hadn't even fought for him as he was fired and evicted.

It wasn't fair. Erron thought he'd had everything: a loving partner, a job he excelled at, and a promising future. All of it scrubbed away without so much as an acknowledgement of regret on Toby's part. A young man and woman walked into the diner and sat at the counter, holding hands the entire time. The ache in his chest twisted deeper. Fucking heteros.

The coffee had long since gone cold, but somehow it tasted better that way, so he waved off the server when she tried to refill the mug. Erron looked at the time glowing in amber numbers on the wall. An hour more, then he'd start his new life.

The door hissed open as an older woman in filthy, tattered clothes shuffled into the diner. The staff ignored her from the moment she stepped across the threshold. Perhaps they knew better than to engage her. Erron was about to follow their example when her gray stare suddenly bore down on him.

With a stern purpose, she strode over to his table. Erron startled when she clamped her dirty hand on his wrist. He pulled back slightly, but her grip was firmer than he expected.

"You've lost someone very close to you." Her voice was raspy, and Erron couldn't help but look into her glassy eyes.

"That's a little vague."

"You're about to travel a great distance." She continued to speak as if she was barely aware of his response.

Erron's brow furrowed. "I *am* in a spaceport."

"Someone will be on board that you thought you'd lost long ago."

Surprise froze Erron in his seat. Gamin was on board. It had been years since they'd laid eyes on one another. Part of the gnawing at his gut was whether Gamin would be happy to see him or not. Erron had given up a long time ago asking his mother about what happened between them. She took the story to her grave. He loved his mother and missed her, but he'd never completely forgiven her for it either.

"You think you've lost the ability to love another, but you'll find it on board once again."

Words refused to form when Erron opened his mouth. A psi on this side of the galaxy? He'd never met one before. Para-humans were few and far between. What were the chances she was telling him his future? She stood silent as he pondered. It wasn't so much that he believed her. Deep down, he just really wanted to.

"Do you see anything else?" Erron's response was timid and quiet.

Her rough voice managed to coo. "Of course, child. It'll cost you ten credits."

Erron's trance was broken by the sound of snickering in the diner. A chubby, greasy man in a gray coverall and cap sat at the counter looking back at him with the broadest grin.

"Myrna's caught another one."

The regulars burst into laughter. Even the old woman still attached to his wrist was beginning to smile. Heat simmered in his face and along the edges of his ears as the others reveled at their inside joke at his expense. He jerked out of Myrna's hold as she cackled. Erron felt so stupid. Of course, she wasn't psychic. She was a practical joker or con artist. It was one of the oldest carnival tricks in history and these people were in on it.

"Sons of bitches can all bugger off."

Snatching his cap off the table, Erron stalked out of the diner, acutely aware of the mocking laughs and stares directed his way. He slammed his hat on his head, crushing his emerald hair as he approached his pallet. Fuming, he checked the straps holding his crates in place with a few rough tugs. Once he was convinced they were secure, he powered up the device. The metal skid hummed to life, floating a half meter from the floor. He grabbed the handle and pulled his pack toward the dock.

If Erron had had any doubts before, they were gone now. He couldn't wait to get off this fucking planet.

ANOTHER HOUR PASSED before anyone arrived at Landing Bay Gamma Seven One to allow Erron access to the dock. He'd been early and wondered how long he'd have to wait. The scene in the diner had ramped up his impatience to an unexpected level. With one hand still towing the skid containing his belongings, Erron straightened his navy-blue cap by the weathered brim. He squared his shoulders as he took a deep breath, waiting for the heavy blast door to ratchet itself open and give him his first look at his future home.

The *Santa Claus* was enormous. The metal hull was dirty and worn but looked powerfully built. It dwarfed the endless landing bay, and Erron was surprised a vessel of this size still landed on-planet instead of shuttling down from orbit. From his research and the captain's conversation, Erron knew the decommissioned ship had once housed over a hundred soldiers while transporting supplies and vehicles. For the thirty or so current members of the crew, it must be fairly spacious. After the civil war, the *Santa Claus* had been purchased by Captain Danverse and populated primarily with a host of men whose military contracts had been bought out after being marked redundant. Since then, they'd traveled the planetary cluster surrounding Alpha Centauri's binary star.

At the far end of the craft, a small group of spaceport workers appeared to be unloading from one of the cargo bays at the ship's rear. Erron didn't see anyone else to ask where he was supposed to go next, so these guys were as good an option as any. As he pulled the anti-grav pallet in the direction of the workers, Erron jumped and skidded himself to a halt as a hatch sprang open near the base of the *Santa Claus*. A set of stairs telescoped to the floor.

A large man chuckled at the top of the steps. "Anxious to get on board?" His head was shaved to the point of stubble, matching the growth framing his jaw. Dark eyes and a wide smile made Erron look twice. Strong and confident as he descended the steps, the man wore a snug T-shirt and breeches lined with pockets down the side. He was thick and muscular with a bit of padding around the waist. Obviously, the man knew his way around the gym but enjoyed his food as well.

"Just a little." Erron laughed. "You must be Sergeant Jacks."

His heavy boots touched down as he took Erron's smaller hand in his own. "Sorry. I'm Corporal Barrus Ryner. Second in command with regards to security. Sergeant Jacks and his partner had an urgent doctor's appointment. It was kind of sudden. You must be the new cook."

"Erron Murfin. Nice to meet you, Corporal Ryner. I hope nothing's wrong with Sergeant Jacks or his partner."

"Call me Barrus. I'm sure he'll be fine. You'll meet Hadrian soon enough and see for yourself. As one of the cooks, you get to meet every one of our little family up close and personal."

Barrus reached into one of the large pockets on his thigh and pulled out a small handheld scanner. He held it up to Erron.

"Sorry. Need a DNA ID before we get any further. Liam will have my hide if I don't follow procedure."

Erron nodded and passed his hand over the device. The panel turned green, and his personal information scrolled over the screen. Barrus scanned the text, no doubt confirming his employment.

"So, Erron. You're single?"

Erron pulled the rim of his cap lower as he tried to hide the heat creeping into his face. There had been a little too much of that lately. "All that info and that's the part that caught your eye?"

The deep bass of Barrus's laugh only made it worse.

"On a ship full of non-heteros, it's always good to know." Barrus stepped over to the skid trailing behind Erron. "This is your stuff? It doesn't seem like very much."

Erron couldn't disguise the wince. The few crates on the pallet were a sad testament to his story. When he had been evicted, he'd barely been given the time to gather what effects he had managed to collect before his ID access had been revoked. Once you added in the items reminding Erron of Toby—that strangely found their way into the incinerator—there wasn't much left of his former life.

"I'm sorry. Did I say something wrong?"

Erron looked up to find a confused security officer in front of him. Barrus cupped Erron's shoulder with a warm hand as his brow twisted in a sad reflection of Erron's memories. It was the first real sympathy he'd received since his dismissal and eviction.

"No. It's just a touchy subject."

"Bad breakup, huh?"

Erron's closed his eyes in embarrassment. "Is that written on my forehead? Captain Danverse said the same thing."

"You're not the first disenfranchised crew member we've ever brought on." Barrus smiled warmly, patting Erron's back. He scratched at his coarse chin as he regarded the skid. "Any idea if this thing can ride up a stairwell? Otherwise, we'll have to go in through the cargo hold, and it's a little crowded with the offloading right now."

"It's held up this long somehow. Let's give it a shot."

With a little work, the pair managed the skid up the stairs and worked their way to the lift leading to Beta deck and Erron's quarters.

"This is you. Room 235. Your DNA ID is already uploaded so just touch the panel to open the door."

Chewing his lower lip, Erron tried to contain his excitement as he laid a finger on the black access panel next to his door. The door slid open with a heavy hiss, and he took a slow step across the threshold. With the exception of a double-sized bed in one corner and a built-in desk along the outer wall, the room was bare. The metal walls were dull and unadorned but obviously clean. It was a simple, uncluttered blank canvas. Perfect.

"There's plenty of storage in the wall panels and you have refrigerated storage for drinks and snacks. You have complete Subspace Link access, and a connection to an extended library of books and vids is part of the entertainment system. Your security clearance will be limited at this point, and we need to get your voiceprint on file for Mrs. Claus. She's the ship's AI. Once we get you set up, there will be a number of things we have to do to get you indoctrinated. We don't ship out for another five days, but I figured you'd want to unpack first before we get into of that."

"What? We don't start with the ritual spankings?"

Barrus laughed out loud. "You're gonna get along fine here."

"Actually, I was wondering if I could see the kitchen. I can unpack any time, and let's be honest"—Erron looked back at the pallet hovering in the hallway—"it's not going to take that long."

Barrus shrugged. "All right. I suppose I'd better get you acquainted with how to get to work. Meals are serious business around here."

"I can tell. You're a big boy. It looks like you can put away quite a bit in one sitting."

"I believe in enjoying everything that's set in front of me." For a moment, Barrus's smile was almost...hungry? For green-haired men? "Come on. I'll take you on the tour."

Erron took a proper moment to assess the security officer. He was a little rough around the edges but charming. Erron was fairly sure Barrus was flirting, but his experience with Toby had left him doubting his instincts. It would be nice to get some honest attention for a change.

"It's good to get you in here now so you won't get mobbed by the crew. They do love the new boys."

Erron laughed out loud. "I bet."

"I can't wait to introduce you to James. I think you two will hit it off well."

"James?"

"My husband. The ship's supply officer. You'll work with him a lot to maintain food inventories and budgets."

Barrus's husband. Of course. The chatting was completely harmless. It was probably for the best anyways. The last thing Erron needed was a romance before he'd even gotten off planet. *Eyes up and off his ass, Erron.* He called himself ridiculous as they exited the lift and headed for the mess hall.

"The kitchen's this way."

Erron followed his escort through the rows of simple dining tables and around the empty food-service counter. With the crew on leave, no meal prep was required and there wasn't any real expectation of running into anyone else. It gave him a chance to absorb his new surroundings. Erron wished a private inspection of the facility were possible but thought it too soon to expect Barrus to let him run around unsupervised. He could save that for another time.

When they rounded the open doorway into the galley, Erron stopped. Standing in front of an open cupboard, there he was.

"Gamin." Erron's word held no volume, cut silent by a loss of breath to power it.

He was bigger than Erron remembered and a little rounder. It suited him. His big, beefy frame matched the tight close crop of his hair and beard peppered with gray. Erron's mouth dried as his nerves sizzled. Engrossed in what looked like an inventory list on his com, he had yet to notice the pair's entrance.

Barrus broke the quiet. "Gamin, I have someone here for you to meet."

Gamin looked up from his work and his face shifted in confusion. Anxious heat rose in Erron's chest as the chef stood up tall and his expression flattened. It was impossible to read what he was thinking. How long had it been? Was taking this position a giant mistake? Gamin's focus was fixed on Erron. He didn't know what to make of it.

"Erron?" Gamin's voice had the same warm rumble he remembered, bringing back a host of memories, good and bad. All of them made him feel like a little kid again.

Barrus looked between the two. "You two know each other?"

"It's been a few years." The tremor in his Erron's voice came out on its own as Gamin walked toward him.

"More than a few."

Erron wanted to wither as Gamin approached. The man was large enough the last time he saw him, and years later, he still dwarfed him.

Gamin blinked over and over, struggling to say something. "How's your mom, Erron?"

"She died in a raid during the war."

Gamin frowned. "Shit. I'm really sorry to hear it. What are you doing here?"

Barrus pointed a thumb at Erron. "Erron's your new cook, Gamin."

Gamin looked vaguely dumbstruck. "You're going to be living on board?"

Erron nodded, feeling the deep crease between his eyes. Perhaps this wasn't the most brilliant plan. Gamin looked almost menacing as he towered over him. He felt lost again, like when Toby had turned on him, and this time there was no other option. He had nowhere else to go. Erron wanted to find a hole and cry himself into it.

Without warning, Gamin snatched Erron into a crushing hug that pushed his hat to the floor.

"I missed you so much, boy." Speaking into Erron's temple, Gamin's voice was coarse and his arms shook. "I thought I'd never lay eyes on you again."

Caught by surprise, it took Erron a few moments to register what was really happening. When he did, he buried himself in the powerful embrace and returned it in kind. Surrounded by warmth and Gamin's comforting arms, Erron tried not to burst into tears. His long-lost father figure had welcomed him home.

Gamin pulled back and kissed Erron squarely on the forehead. "I can't believe you're here." He squeezed Erron tighter as his words were sauced with a belly of laughter. His smile was so radiant, he looked ready to explode.

"For the foreseeable future." Erron was so relieved.

"We just got him on board. Do you want to finish his tour, Gamin? We came straight here from his quarters." Barrus's comment startled Erron. So engrossed in the reunion, he'd half forgotten about his escort. Turning to answer Barrus, Erron found him misty-eyed, grinning as he watched the two.

"You wouldn't mind?"

Barrus shook his head. "You two look like you have some catching up to do. Gamin can com me when you're finished so we can take care of the bureaucratic stuff."

Gamin beamed. "Thank you, Barrus. I'll make sure there's something special for you on the next meal service. Something sweet."

"See? Everybody wins." Barrus waved as he strode out of the mess hall. "Go ahead, boys. I'll see you later."

Gamin shifted until he stood at Erron's side, an arm around his shoulder, as they watched Barrus exit. He kept pressing into him and Erron's fears washed away in such a rush it left him wheezing.

"Are you all right?" Gamin palmed the side of Erron's face. "What's the matter?"

Erron flushed at the paternal attention. "I was afraid you didn't want to see me."

"Never." Gamin pulled him back into the hug. "You just startled me. I couldn't believe it was you. The green hair threw me a little, but I like it. It matches your eyes."

With a roaring laugh bordering on giddy, Gamin embraced Erron, lifting him off his feet, then set him back down. Erron never remembered being this happy before. Not even with Toby. This was a good thing. Once again alongside Erron, Gamin ushered him around the kitchen.

"Okay, boy. Let's show you around. There's a lot to see in your new home. Welcome to the *Santa Claus*."

Chapter Two

"SO THIS USED to be a military vessel?" Erron asked.

After he'd arrived yesterday, they'd spent the day touring the ship and catching up. Because of his arrival, Gamin had never finished stocking. Erron had offered to help, eager to start. Gamin was hesitant to put him to work so soon, but Erron insisted.

Gamin nodded as he shoved an empty box aside with his foot. "Yep. The captain purchased it after his military contract got bought out after the civil war. Most of the men on board are ex-military. A ship this size normally houses over a hundred men or so. There's a lot more breathing room with the smaller crew, makes it easier to live on."

The inventory scanner in Erron's hand reminded him of the devices he'd used in almost every restaurant in which he'd ever worked. A packing list scrolled over the screen as he checked off each item as it found its way into the proper storage. A series of empty cases littered the kitchen floor as Gamin opened another. A few hours had passed as they cataloged the new shipment, verifying the manifest. Perishables were stowed first, meats in the walk-in freezer, vegetables and other fragile produce in the stasis locker, and now they were organizing the dry goods.

"Why'd you sign on?"

Gamin shrugged without stopping. "I think I did like a lot of us. The war was ugly. We all saw things we'd like to forget. The government barely acknowledged our service and it seemed like most of the survivors weren't happy with the presence of soldiers. It was hard. Too many bad memories and too much bad blood. Life is better off planet. We know what the rules are and what's expected of us." Gamin handed Erron a pair of canisters. "Put that in the pantry over there."

Following Gamin's finger, Erron found the home for the seasoning over the prep counter. Gamin had insisted Erron's first duty to be learning the layout and where everything belonged. It made sense. Apparently, they ordered and received new shipments of foodstuffs at every port.

"Were you drafted like I was?"

"Oh yeah. That made it a little easier coming home, but not by much. I think it was hardest for the career military like Danverse and Liam Jacks." Gamin set a series of cartons on the table. "Dry pasta. Tall pantry."

"I was drafted but ended up as a company cook. I never saw any real action." Erron ticked each type of pasta off the list and added them to the appropriate shelf.

"You were lucky. As a trained chef, the military's infinite wisdom stuck me as an infantry foot soldier."

Erron grimaced. "That's awful."

"Yes, it was."

"I guess it didn't take much to convince you to come on board."

Gamin paused, searching his memory. "It did, actually. Danverse recruited me after doing a search through the personnel files of the discharges. He wanted someone to handle the kitchen on board. I kept saying no, but he talked me into interviewing on the ship. The man is very persuasive."

"No shit."

Gamin tossed the empty crate aside and opened another. "I figured I'd go through the motions and let him down easy. Be polite. Make a graceful exit. Then he showed me the kitchen. It was horrible. The whole place was filthy and most of the appliances were obsolete. Half of the burners on the main cooker were out. It was unusable."

"Then why did you stay?"

"At the time, the whole crew were veterans. They fought and bled for their government and were cast aside. They deserved better than what they got. Danverse let me refit the kitchen as I needed. He's always been generous with the budget. He told me the men lived on the *Santa Claus* and he wanted it to be a new home for everyone on board."

"Do you think the captain knew you'd say yes after you saw the condition of the kitchen?"

Gamin snorted. "I wouldn't put it past him." Reading the labels as he went, Gamin made a tower of boxes, reminding Erron of giant children's blocks. "At first, I thought I'd get things running smoothly and be on my way, but I never quite found the reason to leave. The crew became my new family. They're good men for the most part, even if they're a little rough-edged. You'll see." With a quick hand, Gamin dismantled the tower and shuffled everything into its place. "You know, Erron, you never really told me why you joined up."

Erron's cheeks warmed, and he turned away. He knew the details of how he came on board would come up eventually—it wasn't exactly a secret—but did it have to happen so soon? Of all people to tell, Gamin should have been the easiest, but the extended pause gave him away.

He stamped down the stupidity. Gamin was the last man to judge others. Even after so many years, he sounded and acted the same as Erron remembered him. He could be trusted. But it didn't mean Erron was ready to go into exacting detail either.

"Didn't have a whole lot of choice, really. Had a horrible breakup and found myself with no job, no home, and no friends or family to speak of." Erron took a deep breath. Telling the abbreviated version still made his pulse race. "It took a while to get myself together enough to look for work, and my funds started to run out. I got lucky with the *Santa Claus*'s advert. I checked out the public details and kind of freaked out when I saw you were part of the crew. I guess it just seemed like the right thing to do."

"You looked a little nervous when you came on yesterday."

Erron's breath escaped with a bark of laughter. "Are you kidding? I was ready to piss myself. I had no idea how you were going to react."

"Me either. The captain didn't tell me who the new cook was, just that he hired someone. You both surprised the hell out of me."

"Well, it has been a long time."

Gamin stopped his work and focused solely on Erron, his voice tinged with regret. "Yes, it has. And it shouldn't have been. You were family long before the crew ever was. I won't put that kind of distance between us again. I promise."

"That works for me, Gamin." A warmth filled Erron, calming the anxious edge, and bringing a smile to his face. The echo on Gamin's face only made it better.

"Let's finish stashing these supplies. Looks like there's only four cases left. We can watch a vid tonight and catch up. The main crew won't be back for a few days, so we don't have to sort the menus out right away. It'll give us a chance to make up for some lost time."

"I like the sound of that."

With a fresh enthusiasm, Gamin tore into the remaining containers, and Erron kept right along with him. It was clear Gamin wouldn't go easy on Erron, but he looked forward to it. He knew Gamin would hold his promise to keep close as long as it was physically possible. The conviction in his vow was unmistakable.

What a shame they'd been apart for so long. Gamin was Erron's sole role model as his mother tried with little success to find a permanent mate in her life. When Erron was seven, Gamin had explained where babies came from because his mother was incapable of finding the courage. Gamin had taught Erron to shave. When he turned fourteen, Gamin had had to explain how boys played with other boys. Again, his mother had been mortified, talking to her son about the subject. Stacy Murfin loved her son, Erron had no doubt, but certain subjects came with undebatable boundaries for her.

Erron had grown up in Gamin's absence. Both men were different, but the fundamental persons were still there. He only wished he knew what had driven Gamin away. Erron's mother had never answered him when asked, changing the subject at every opportunity. He'd learned to stop asking.

Thinking of his mother always made him somber. Layered with the sting of Toby's betrayal, it soured the thought further. He wanted to ask Gamin what his mother kept to herself, but he needed happy thoughts now. Better to save that conversation for another day. He was on board the *Santa Claus* and he had Gamin back in his life. Whatever happened before was unimportant. It was time to start fresh.

With a husky cheer, Gamin put away the last canister and wiped his hands on his pants. "That's everything."

One last pass over the scanner list and Erron confirmed the job was done. His first assignment as a part of the crew went exactly as it should. It was good to be in a kitchen again. Job complete, Erron found Gamin pulling a face as he sniffed himself.

"All right. Let's get cleaned up. You don't want to hang out with me when I'm this rank. We can come back here later and I'll knock together a meal before we choose a vid."

"Sounds perfect."

Outside the mess hall, Gamin clasped a heavy hand on Erron's shoulder. "Good work, by the way." He gave Erron a playful shake. "I guess we'll have to keep you."

Not much was said as they made their way to Beta deck. Erron's chest lightened as they rode the lift. Life had the possibility to be good here. Stepping out into the hallway, they stopped in front of Erron's door, and Gamin gestured to the communal area in the center of the living quarters.

"Go get your kit and meet me in the lockers."

"See you there."

Beta deck was situated like a large dormitory. The rooms ran in a loop with a central facility containing a gymnasium, lockers, lavatories, and shower room. On a non-hetero vessel, the layout was dubious to say the least.

Since the majority of the crew was off ship, Erron bolstered his nerve enough to enter the locker room. In his quarters, he'd stalled for a bit, deciding how to proceed. What was considered normal on the *Santa Claus*? Did the men walk around half-dressed? Less than half? There were a lot of factors in fitting into an established community. Towel over his shoulder, he stepped through the doorway into the locker room. The gymnasium lurked down one end and the shower room was visible down the other. He wondered what games were possible with a dozen men stripped down and showering together in one room together. The likelihood for something tawdry to happen seemed high.

Clothes lay over the bench and the sound of water running told Erron Gamin had beaten him there. Not surprising really, Gamin had been on the ship for years. This was his home, and Erron hoped he'd soon feel the same.

Stripping off, Erron dropped pieces of his outfit in the same fashion as Gamin's. Peeling off his briefs, a sudden surge of awkwardness came over him. He was about to get in the shower with Gamin. A nervous giggle tried to rip out of his mouth, so he choked it down. He was being childish.

"Took you long enough." Gamin didn't look in Erron's direction, holding his head under the spray as Erron entered.

"I had to find my towel."

Erron hung his towel on the hook near the doorway and selected a shower with a buffer of one nozzle between them. The control panel beeped as Erron touched it, but nothing happened. Over and over, he touched the pad only to be mocked by the same tone.

"It's voice activated." Gamin barely glanced over his shoulder. "Just tell it the temperature you want."

Erron's face heated up. He refused to admit he couldn't muster the nerve to use the shower the night before after they'd turned in. The ship was too quiet and too new.

Ducking his head slightly, Erron leaned forward and spoke to the black panel. "Forty-two degrees Celsius." A torrent of heated water rushed over Erron. The delicious heat the first step in washing away months of grime and sad reminders of his derailed life. The cheap inns he'd been forced to rent after being evicted had lousy facilities. This...this was a small piece of chocolate decadence.

"Like your showers pretty hot?" Gamin continued to face the wall as he soaked himself.

Erron angled his hips, keeping his privates out of view. "I'd forgotten how nice it feels."

For the first time in decades, Erron was self-conscious. The fitness membership had expired shortly after the breakup, but Erron hadn't lost too much tone. He'd never be large and imposing. His frame didn't allow it, but a lean body and smooth skin still turned heads. The treatment responsible for his hair growing in green made the rest on his body the same color. Jade-colored hair on his arms and legs was too weird, and a green pubic zone was the mark of a perverted clown, so it had had to go. There was nothing wrong with him, but why he needed to hide himself, he couldn't say. He certainly never acted this shy in front of the troops during the war. It was more than a bit hypocritical when he peered over his shoulder at his showering partner.

Tall and thick with coarse hair on his arms and legs, Gamin's size and sturdiness were a stark contrast to Erron's smaller stature. Wisps of fur reached around the sides of Gamin's rounded belly that matched the meaty globes of his behind. Everything about him was solid and manly. The heavy dusting of gray on his head and beard fit him as well.

It was true, he probably shouldn't be looking, but Erron had never seen Gamin undressed in all those years. Not even shirtless at the park when he was growing up. From what he saw, the view wasn't half bad. Gamin had nothing to be ashamed of. What he did notice was how deliberate Gamin was being at not looking at him.

"You're a lot bigger than I remembered." Erron couldn't help watching Gamin soap his body while continuing to face the wall. It had been a long while since he'd had an opportunity to be with a man. It wasn't his plan to be with Gamin. It's not why he was here in the first place. As long as Gamin didn't turn around, Erron could enjoy the show regardless of the twinge of dirty guilt. He prayed Gamin kept his eyes turned away. That might be hard to explain and only a little bit mortifying.

"Yeah well, I've had time to eat a few good meals."

"It looks good on you."

Gamin chuckled as lines of lazy suds followed the contours of his back and between the crevice of his haunches. "Thanks. You've changed a lot over the years too."

"I'm not a kid anymore."

"No. No, you're not," Gamin said, drenching his head under the spray.

"YOU GOT EVERYTHING stashed away? Stuff tends to shift during launch."

Erron answered Gamin's question with a tight nod. What little he owned was safely stowed, but he hedged in a circle unable to settle. Sharp fingers of anxiety tickled his spine, bringing a tightness to his chest.

"The *Santa Claus* is preparing for launch. All passengers and personnel, please proceed to designated departure seating." Mrs. Claus's voice was unable to blunt Erron's nerves.

Gamin patted his shoulder. "That's us."

Erron had to be nearly pushed out of his room. The door closing was a signal of his old life being left behind. He wasn't sure if he was prepared yet, but he pressed his hand uneasily to the black panel, locking his quarters.

A chorus of mechanical whirs echoed in every direction. Panels hissed open down the corridors as seats rotated out of their hiding places. In rapid-fire succession, each locked into position with an audible *thunk* of metal like prison bars slamming shut. One after another, the noise ratcheted Erron's discomfort higher and higher.

Once the racket stopped, Erron followed Gamin to a row of seats. Every chair sported a solid framework and harnessing like an amusement park ride. The image didn't grant Erron a sensation of safety. He used to puke on roller coasters.

"This is some serious hardware. Are we preparing to crash?" Erron gripped the metal cage and tried to shake it loose.

"Priest is a good pilot. He manages to only rough us up a little bit."

"Is that supposed to make me feel better?"

Gamin snickered. "You need to relax. The seats are just a precaution. We're perfectly safe."

Erron didn't feel perfectly safe. Why, he had no idea. Everything looked ready to withstand a crash landing at full speed, but it didn't calm him. Gamin was forced to grab him by the shoulders and usher him into his seat. The large brace swung down over his head and connected into the framework between his legs. Once it engaged, Gamin turned a handle next to Erron's thigh and pushed it into place.

"What was that lever for?"

"Manual lock. We don't automate everything."

The restraints weighed on Erron's shoulders and chest but refused to move when Gamin tested them. With a satisfied nod, he climbed into his own seat.

"Are you comfortable? Nothing pinching you?"

"No, I'm fine."

Down the hall, a few crew members latched themselves in. He recognized Barrus and another blond man he guessed to be James. Barrus noticed Erron, turned and whispered to his husband. Both men gave a polite nod and wave. Erron returned the gesture but kept noticing so many vacant chairs. Not even half in this section were being used.

"Why are there so many empty seats?" A shiver raced over Erron as he pictured an explosive decompression sucking half the crew out into the airless vacuum.

Gamin pulled his own safety harness into position and locked himself in. "The ship was built for over three times the number of people on board now. We're not trying to fill to capacity. This is normal. Relax."

"The *Santa Claus* will be launching in T minus five minutes and counting."

Erron took long, slow breaths as he passed the endless minutes waiting for the inevitable. There was a sense of adventure and excitement inside him over leaving Alpha Centauri and all the nonsense behind, but it was being salted with apprehension. The harness was padded and comfortable, restricting his movements, but it didn't stop Erron from trying to rattle the contraption loose.

"The *Santa Claus* will begin launch in five...four..."

"Are you ready?" Gamin asked.

"Three...two..."

"I think so."

"One...launch."

A roar built around them filled with sound and tremors building to the cadence of a runaway rocket. Pressure flattened Erron into the seat. Vibrations shivered through his skeleton. What was that sound? Was the ship breaking up? Crushing his eyes closed, he gripped his restraints, praying they held. His breathing soughed through his teeth in quick hisses.

Gamin raised his voice over the cacophony as he stroked Erron's hair off his clammy forehead. "Are you all right? You look a little pale."

Erron didn't respond but tightened his fingers, the steadfast metal in his hands resisting his attempts to crush it.

Gamin clasped Erron's shoulder. "You're going to be fine. It's always a little rough until we clear the atmosphere."

"I've never been off-world before."

"There's a first time for everything."

Erron opened his eyes, his voice shaking worse than the vessel. "Oh God. I'm leaving my home. What have I done?"

"You're starting over. On your terms."

Gamin pried Erron's hand from its death grip on the harness and squeezed their palms together. The warmth was a lifeline. It traveled up his arm, smoothing out the roughest edges of his fear.

"If it's what you want, I'm going to help you make this home. I'll take care of you."

Erron clutched Gamin's hand tighter. "You promise?"

"I promise." With their hands locked together, Gamin didn't appear concerned or angry. He looked pleased to be saying it.

As fast as it came, the roar leveled down to a soft hum and the quaking dissipated to nothing. The *Santa Claus* must have escaped the atmosphere.

SINCE THE LAUNCH occurred early enough, a dinner meal service was in order. Everything had been prepped in advance, so little needed to be done other than serve, giving Erron an opportunity to meet the crew. It was too bad he didn't enjoy it more. Cook and chef both made apologies to the men over Erron's visible discomfort. He had yet to shake off the effects of the launch. The crew members seemed understanding as they welcomed Erron on board. It didn't take long to see how much respect the men gave Gamin for taking care of them so well.

The meal service came and went, and Erron continued being edgy and nauseous. While not laced with panic like the actual launch, he couldn't stop the unease. He skipped his own food, the thought unappealing. Gamin ate a sandwich before the final cleanup, keeping a watchful eye over Erron as they sat after hours in the quiet kitchen.

"You sure you don't want anything to eat?"

Erron shook his head. "No, thank you. It just sounds like a bad idea right now."

"Are you okay?"

"I'm fine. Let's just get the last of the dishes in the sanitizer so I can go lay down. I'll be better after I rest."

"If you want, I can finish up."

"No. I can wash a few dishes. I'm not an invalid." Erron pushed himself to his feet and the world spun, causing his stomach to roll. Losing his balance, he crashed into the table's edge, a sharp pain lancing his hip. Gamin jumped up and caught Erron when his feet buckled, unable to find a stable hold on the floor.

"Oh God…" A sickening urge came over Erron. He shoved out of Gamin's arms, barely making it to the sink on his clumsy feet before his stomach emptied itself. Erron was dry heaving before it finally stopped. Gamin turned on the cold water, rinsed the sink, and applied a cool cloth to the back of Erron's neck.

"Feeling any better?"

Erron's breaths were hard and labored. "My head won't stop spinning. I don't think I can stand."

"This isn't right. I'm taking you to sick bay."

"I don't want to go to sick bay." Erron's protests proved a waste of time as everything spun once again, until he found himself slung over Gamin's shoulder.

"Don't puke on me."

Closing his eyes, Erron tried to ignore the indignity of the moment. There was little choice in the matter. "No promises."

Gamin kept a steadying hand on Erron, which gave him something to concentrate on instead of the bounce of Gamin's rushed footsteps or the swells of vertigo. The trip was shorter than he had expected, ending at the sound of a pair of doors swishing open.

"Hey, Doc! We could use a hand here."

"Set him down there and let me get a scan on him."

Erron drifted like a leaf in the wind until he settled onto the bed. Daring to open his eyes, he found a slender, blond man with a serious expression looking over him with a keen eye. Erron found if he stayed motionless, the swimming sensation minimized itself.

"Welcome to sick bay, Mr. Murfin. I'm Dr. Bosch. What's going on?"

Gamin answered. "He can't stand upright and started throwing up."

The doctor paused, gave a calculated glance at Gamin's proximity, and returned to Erron.

"Is this right, Erron?" Erron gave him the smallest nod, trying hard not to set off another wave of nausea.

"Did it just happen? Or have your symptoms been coming for a while?"

Gamin answered for him again. "Erron's been off since the launch."

Dr. Bosch's brow flattened a bit and paused. Taking a small breath, he continued. "Since the launch?"

"I told you that's what happened!"

Setting his scanner on the bed, Dr. Bosch stood up straight, the air of authority radiating off the man in spite of his smaller stature. He aimed a withering glare right in Gamin's face, which was the only option considering how the chef crowded the doctor. Gamin practically growled through his gritted teeth.

"Gamin, I understand you're concerned. But one of the bonuses of being the head medical officer practicing on board the *Santa Claus* is that I don't have to deal with overprotective mothers telling me how to do my job every time their children have the sniffles. If I ever find the need to cook a five-course meal for a party of fifty, I'll be sure to ask for your help. Until then, please be quiet and let me examine Erron on my own, or I'll sedate you so hard you'll be hallucinating in the corner for the next week."

Gamin looked ready to explode. Red-faced, he trembled with frustration, shifting forward in some kind of dominance display. Dr. Bosch stood his ground, unaffected and somehow taller than before. Never raising his voice, the doctor's commanding tone bore an edge of steel. There was no doubt who was in charge of sick bay. The way Gamin stepped back and huffed, he knew it too. Bosch picked his scanner up again and passed it over Erron as he resumed his exam.

"Are you feeling dizzy, Erron? A tingling sensation through your extremities?"

Erron's voice sounded frail. "Yes, sir."

"Oh, aren't you a polite one? Let's hope the rest of the crew doesn't rub off on you." After a few passes with the device, Bosch fixated on the readout.

"Am I gonna live, Doc?"

The doctor chuckled. "You can't get out of feeding us that easily. You're just experiencing side effects from the ship's artificial gravity well. Some people are more sensitive to it than others. Hold tight. I'll get you something to settle you."

The doctor walked out of Erron's line of vision. He made a point not to move a muscle since he was afraid to turn his head and risk setting off a new wave of vomiting. Shortly, the doctor returned with a new medical tool in his hand. He touched a series of controls and placed it to Erron's neck. A small pinch and hiss and a cooling sensation emanated from the injection site. It swept over his body, taking the nausea and vertigo with it.

"Oh, Doc, that's much better already."

"Stay still. Give it a chance to work. That dose was only a short-term blocker. Assuming you signed the standard work contract, you're going to be with us for a while. From the severity of your symptoms and your scan, you'll need a regular dosing to counteract the effects. I'll synthesize your prescription. One pill a day in the morning when you wake up."

"For how long?"

"For a few months at least, until your body adjusts."

"Is there a chance it won't?"

"It's possible, but that's pretty rare. I'll send the pharmacological file to your private com. We'll monitor your progress as we go. All right, why don't we have you sit up and see how you're doing."

Gingerly, Erron shifted to a seated position, wary of an impending wave of sickness. Once upright, he was fine. Worn from the stress of the day, perhaps, but feeling more human than earlier.

Gamin ran a hand over the back of Erron's head. "Doing better?"

Erron nodded. The tension released through Gamin's touch, matching the quiet exhale. He'd been worried.

"Can I go now?"

"Oh no. I haven't done my basic workup on you yet, Erron. You were scheduled in two days, but since I have you here, we might as well take advantage of the opportunity. Assuming *your mother* will allow it?"

Gamin flashed a smirk of sarcasm. "Very funny, Doc."

"Oh good. Then you'll understand when I tell you to sit down out of my way while I take care of my patient."

"I'll be okay, Gamin."

Gamin continued to hover. "Can I wait for him?"

"Yes, Gamin. But you'll need to step back so I can draw the privacy screens. This is not a peep show."

Gamin's eyes went huge. "I would never—"

"This shouldn't take too long, Gamin. Thank you for bringing Erron in so quickly."

Erron suppressed a laugh at the doctor's comment and Gamin's shock. Wasting no time, Dr. Bosch pulled the privacy panels around the bed, herding Gamin out of his workspace.

"All right, Erron. Let's start your medical panel."

THE EXAMINATION WAS less invasive than Erron expected but infinitely thorough. Dr. Bosch treated him with total professionalism and left no square centimeter of his body unscanned or unprobed. Bosch made it clear he expected Erron back in sick bay on a weekly basis as part of being a new recruit, or more often if he deemed it necessary. The doctor's dedication to his role on board eased some of Erron's concerns.

"You didn't have to escort me back to my quarters."

Gamin traced his hand over the small of Erron back. "I wanted to make sure you were all right."

The pair made a slow trek back to Beta deck and approached Erron's door. As embarrassed as he was, Erron was thankful Gamin had been present. It was the first time in a while Erron had someone he could count on. After the fiasco with Toby, it was a refreshing change.

"I should go back to the kitchen and help finish cleaning up."

"Don't worry about that. I'll take care of it. You just get some rest."

"But, Gamin—"

"I said rest."

Erron sighed in defeat. "Yes, sir."

Gamin placed a small kiss on Erron's head and hugged him carefully. "I'll come get you in the morning for breakfast prep. Have a good night."

"Good night, Gamin."

Gamin stood in the hall until the door closed between them, leaving Erron alone in his room. He was better but exhausted. It had been a stressful day. The monitor over his desk signaled a private message. He'd barely been there long enough to know anyone. Who would be mailing him? The lone message in his in-box was from Dr. Bosch. No doubt the medical packet he had mentioned earlier. Erron tapped the screen and opened the file.

"You've gotta be kidding me, Doc."

A small novella of non-laymen medical fine print littered the screen. Page after page of documentation made his eyes hurt. How long was this document? He'd had enough of feeling like crap for one day. Erron turned off the screen and climbed into bed without bothering to remove his clothes. He'd read it later when he had the energy. Right then, the only thing he cared about was bringing the day to an end and starting over fresh.

Chapter Three

"THREE WEEKS ON board. Are you getting settled in okay?"

Erron nodded to James as they continued the inventory in the galley's pantry. "I kind of freaked at first, but it's not so bad. It's a nice change of scenery."

"It's always like that at first. Before you know it, being off ship will feel really strange."

"You're probably right."

Finding a rhythm to the *Santa Claus*'s lifestyle took a little getting used to. Being the new guy, finding a niche in the crew's family-work relationship was proving to be a little daunting. Not that Erron wasn't trying, but preparing three meals a day for the crew was a harder workload than he'd anticipated. Every evening, they chatted on the walk back to his quarters with Gamin thanking him for his hard work. Afterward, he'd fall asleep in his clothes almost as soon as he walked inside.

But he loved it. Finally being alongside Gamin again was like the last several years without him had never happened. The panic he had experienced during the launch abated quickly, and Gamin was kind enough not to mention it. Erron had forgotten how much he'd missed the man's presence, how he had inspired him to learn to cook. Now that he was on the ship with him, he wished he'd found a way on board sooner.

The labor was becoming easier, and Erron was finding time to have actual chats with members of the crew while serving meals. Barrus and his husband, James, had spent more time than anyone else extending a friendly hand in welcome to Erron. They seemed to understand how hard this new way of life was, and it was helping Erron adjust.

Barrus and James were good together. Slightly mismatched, Barrus was large, wide, and slightly gruff to James's lean and well-kept appearance. Watching them brought a small pang of jealousy over Erron. The pair were so comfortable together, far more than Erron had been with Toby when he believed all was well. They were good-natured, helpful, and had a bawdy sense of humor. Since the two of them were a couple, Erron dismissed their tawdry jokes as just that: jokes. Toby's betrayal had left deep scars, and Erron was hardly believing anyone would find him attractive at the moment. The fake fortune-teller from the diner on Alpha Centauri was full of shit. He wasn't looking for love. He simply wanted to start his life over and fit in.

James explained how as the supply officer, he was involved in every aspect of acquisitions and material accounting and budgeting. He was responsible for all inventories that didn't involve client shipments and the occasional passenger manifests. That day he was working with Erron to verify food supplies needing to be restocked at the next spaceport. Usually Gamin was in charge of this task, but he wanted Erron to know everything inside the galley. It was his home and responsibility for the foreseeable future.

James scrolled through his list. "There's a few more things to check off. What's left on the top shelf?"

Erron grabbed the small step stool and planted it in front of the large open storage panel. The shelves were fairly well stocked, but they'd stacked items too high and he was just a little too short to get a proper look at the top shelf. He climbed up the miniature ladder to inventory the hiding dry goods and his vision spun. A wave of vertigo hit him as gravity upended itself and the ladder was no longer under his foot. He braced for impact but found himself caught in James's arms. He might have been leaner than Barrus, but the man was strong and, damn it, he smelled good.

"Are you okay?" James's handsome face, short blond hair, brown eyes, and manicured jaw came back into focus as Erron's dizziness faded. He wished it was possible to reverse the rush of warmth blushing his skin. If he could stop doing that, it would only be too soon.

"I'm fine." Erron stood up with a slight wobble that was already sorting itself. Turning away from James, he nervously straightened his clothing.

"This is your first time off-planet, isn't it?"

Erron's brow flattened as he ground his teeth. "Yes."

"It's okay." James placed a friendly hand on Erron's shoulder. "The artificial gravity messes with people sometimes. Inner-ear disturbances and all that nonsense. Have you seen Dr. Bosch yet?"

Erron rolled his eyes. "Oh yeah. The first time happened not long after we got out of orbit. Gamin rushed me to sick bay. It was humiliating. I felt like a five-year-old again."

"Gamin's just protective. What did the doctor say?"

"I'll be fine." Erron shrugged. "He says it's fairly normal and has me on some meds to acclimate me. This was the first spell in three days. Bosch says it will gradually disappear completely. Don't tell Gamin about this. He'll badger me back to sick bay."

James smiled. "If you say so, I'll keep quiet. But let me know if anything else happens. I don't want you to get hurt."

"Thanks." Part of the grin on Erron's face was simply the weight of James's hand on his shoulder. The pressure of his palm was a welcome sensation he'd missed since Toby left. Toby had been a tactile lover. Excellent hands. A flood of useless and painful memories came forward. Erron took a peripheral glance at James's hand as the smile flattened. James must have noticed. With a stuttered movement, the contact was gone.

"I'll finish the top shelf." With a soft clearing of his throat, James climbed the step stool and peered into the back of the top shelf. Guilt filled Erron at once. It was nice for someone to care for a change and here he was reacting negatively to a simple friendly gesture. Sure, he'd been hugged many times by Gamin since arriving, but they'd known each other for decades. In spite of the rumors about James's sordid reputation amongst the men, he'd done nothing Erron should have been alarmed over. Toby had done some serious damage to Erron, but it had nothing to do with James.

Erron sighed and was about to apologize when James spoke up.

"Are you staring at my ass? I swear I can sense this heat on me."

The laugh and the blush burst out simultaneously from Erron, and his guilt dissipated. If it was James's intention, he gave him high marks for execution. The unmanly giggle threatening to erupt came to a stop when Gamin appeared, watching the pair with his hands on his hips.

"Are you harassing my cook, James? I thought you'd learned your lesson after Hadrian trounced you in the shower that one time."

"I'll have you know he felt very sorry about that. He apologized and everything."

Gamin chuckled. "I bet."

Erron smiled at Gamin. "James and I were just finishing the inventory."

James stepped down and ticked off the last items on his com pad.

"I almost forgot, Erron. Priest, one of the pilots, is hosting a poker game tonight. We need a sixth. If you can tear yourself away from Gamin for the night, we'd like you to come. Fifty credits to join the game."

"Poker?" Erron perked up at the word. "I haven't played poker in a long time."

"This better not be one of your initiation pranks." Gamin's paternal grumble was unmistakable.

James paused for a moment, his head tilting slightly to follow Gamin's remark. He placed a penitent hand over his heart and raised his right hand. "No, it's not. I promise. I'd say 'on my honor,' but we know what a joke that is." Reaching out with a single index finger, he poked Gamin in the chest. "Erron needs to mingle with the rest of our rowdy asses. You've monopolized him long enough."

A poker game sounded great to Erron. "I'm in."

"Perfect. I'll come get you around 20:30 hours." James looked to Gamin with a mocking plea. "Will that be okay with you, sir? I promise to get Erron home before curfew." He cast a wink at Erron. "We promise there won't be a hazing with wooden paddles or anything."

Gamin laughed as he cuffed James along the ear. "Shut up. Erron's a big boy. He can do what he wants." He turned to Erron. "Since you'll be out and about, you can stop by the kitchen around midnight and put the ingredients for breakfast into the thawing unit. The menu list will be on the freezer."

Erron nodded as James smiled.

"Since that's settled, I need to run. I'll see you tonight, Erron."

ERRON COULD BARELY contain his anxiety. This was the first time he'd interacted with any of the crew, other than Gamin, outside of the mess hall. He wanted to fit in but the new social climate left him acting more than a bit awkward. The crew were so comfortable with each other, he wondered if they'd accept him as well. He ran a nervous hand through his hair until James grabbed his wrist and brought it down to his side.

"You're going to be fine. Relax and be yourself. The guys are going to love you."

With a hand to the small of his back, James led Erron into the recreation room. Instead of being the same unfeeling gray metal running through the ship, the room was painted a deep warm rustic red. Thick-cushioned chairs, couches, and beanbags completed the seating area surrounding an enormous vidscreen. A lacquered, black pool table was nestled into the far corner. The four men seated around a sturdy circular table were the only other inhabitants in the room at this hour.

Erron spotted Barrus first. His husky frame barely fitting in his chair, his face lit up when Erron walked through the door. He helped James get things started. If the other men sensed his nervousness, they didn't let on as they took turns introducing themselves. All of them appeared to be thrilled to meet their new crew member. The knot of unease unraveled.

Teddy, the communications officer, wore a sleeveless shirt showing a series of tattoos covering the length of both arms. He sported a tidy beard and his brown hair was tied back into a shoulder-length ponytail. Carson, Dr. Bosch's medical assistant, was a gruff, burly man with dense waves of hair on his head as well as spilling out of the open collar of his unbuttoned thermal shirt. Last, there was the pilot, Priest, who grinned in excitement at Erron's inclusion to the game.

Priest rose from his seat to give Erron a firm handshake. "Glad to see Gamin was able to spare you for a night so we can get a chance to know you a little."

Barrus broke in. "Gamin and Erron haven't seen each other in years. They needed to catch up before cutting Erron loose on the ship with you shameless lot." The small crowd broke into a rumbling chorus of familial laughter. The sound made Erron's mood sing. He could be happy there.

"Well, now that I'm here, let's play some cards."

A roar of approval came over the table as Erron took his seat across from Priest. James sat next to Priest across from Barrus and blew his husband a quick kiss. Carson opened the case on the table and passed out the betting chips while James collected the funds via DNA ID scans using his com pad. Priest pulled out a deck of blank cards sitting in a smooth metal holder. He pressed the control on the edge and filed through the holographic menu that appeared until he found the poker selection. Once chosen, the card surfaces came to life creating a set suitable for the game.

"I just got these babies on our last trip to Luxoria." Priest looked quite proud of his toys.

"That mustn't have been cheap." Teddy whistled as he inspected the shiny stand.

Priest rubbed his hands together and picked up the deck. "I'm planning to earn the cost back from you suckers tonight."

Once everyone was set, he dealt the cards.

"Straight-up poker, nothing wild. House rules are in effect. Ante up, boys." White chips bounced into the center of the table as the game began.

It had been a long time since Erron played poker, but he was no stranger to the game. Due to his skill, a fair amount of credits had lined his pockets back in the day, before he met Toby. Normally in an unfamiliar game, he would have asked if there were any house rules, but these were men he'd see every day. He needed to get along with them. Afraid to offend anyone, Erron kept his mouth shut. He surveyed the players as the game progressed. So far, the men were being cautious, but it didn't take long to see the skill levels of his opponents.

Barrus was good at hiding his reactions and played smart. James was scrutinizing every player and watching every card that hit the table. Erron was convinced he was calculating odds and counting cards. Priest seemed a touch reckless in his choices, but still a decent opponent. Teddy and Carson appeared equally matched, but even with varying skill levels, there was always a certain level of luck directing the game.

One odd thing Erron noted was that the players were being overly cautious as the game went on.

Over two and a half hours had gone by and the game had taken a considerable shift. Priest had a sizable pile of chips in front of him while Erron's were down to next to nothing. The rest of the group appeared to be surviving through their careful betting.

It wasn't as if Erron was playing badly. He played every hand the way he'd been taught, the way the odds should favor him, and every time, Priest had the better hand. Most of the pile in front of the man was from Erron's holdings. He was losing fast. The worst thing was how he could see Priest wasn't a better player. He was just a fortunate bastard.

If Lady Luck continued to ignore Erron, he was likely to become a misogynist. Adding Toby's bitch fiancée and the fake gypsy at the diner into the list, it seemed lately like every female connected with Erron was screwing him over these days. Good thing his mother wasn't still around to see this.

Every gram of Erron's skill was necessary to quell his frustration. It was poor form as a player and as a sportsman to start complaining. He wanted to fit in with the crew. The last thing he needed was to be marked as a sore loser.

Priest dealt the next round, and Erron found himself looking at four hearts in his hand, a possible flush. After one round of careful betting, everyone folded except him and Priest. Erron was determined to win back part of his money and not be the first one out of the game.

He traded out one card while Priest replaced three. A fifth heart completed his flush hand with a queen high. The odds of Priest beating him were slim.

"I'll start with fifty." Erron pitched a red chip into the pot.

Priest's eyes narrowed while his sly grin made Erron nervous. He grabbed a stack of blue chips, counted them, and set them in the center.

"I'll see your bet and raise you a thousand."

Erron made a quick count of his stash. "That puts me all in, but I can't cover it. I'm short three hundred fifty."

"Of course you can. Your shirt and pants are worth three hundred a piece." Priest wasn't even trying to hide his glee.

"Come again?"

The grin on Priest's face was far too bright as he explained. "Shirt and pants are worth three hundred. Underwear is worth five. House rules."

"Priest…" James's voice held a clear warning.

"House rules, James. He didn't have to agree to it."

Erron wanted to pound his head on the table for not asking details. He was so intent on being part of the group, he failed to find out what he was getting himself into. The first rule of gambling: never play a man at his own game. Of course no one expected a strip poker game without it being announced.

"It's fine, James. I'm not someone who doesn't follow through." Erron made sure James understood he was fine playing along. "Are there any more of the house rules that I need to know before we continue?"

Priest gave a knowing Cheshire grin to James. "Why don't you tell him, James?" James squirmed in his seat, having trouble looking Erron in the eye. He was clearly not happy to pass along the news. His words were slow and tinged in apology. Or was that guilt?

"Whoever loses and ends up naked spends the night with the winner of the game."

Laughing in disbelief, Erron scrubbed a hand through his hair. What had he gotten himself into? No wonder the men were playing so conservatively. No doubt once someone lost, the game would gain a new level of aggressiveness while the boys combated to be the final winner. This kind of game was probably pretty common. He should have known better, playing poker with a batch of strangers was risky enough, but with someone as sketchy as Priest, it was downright idiotic.

James's guilt got the better of him and he spoke up. "You don't have to do this, Erron. I should have said something when house rules came up."

Priest looked absolutely aghast at James's suggestion. Erron considered letting James stew for a while, but when it came down to it, he really wasn't offended by the house rules. None of the men at the table were unattractive, and he'd been catching furtive glances from each of them since he'd walked through the door. A night with any one of them would be a nice distraction. No matter what the fake gypsy had foretold, he wasn't looking for true love anymore.

Erron grinned. "It's okay, James. Besides, you might actually win."

With a wolfish grin, Erron peeled his shirt over his head, catching the complete attention of every player. As his flat, tight stomach came into view, all conversation stopped. Every male in the room projected his need at Erron without a single syllable. He tossed his shirt into the pot, then unbuckled his pants. A collective gasp went through the room as he peeled his clothing down his lean, taut thighs, depositing it on top of his shirt. Erron stood before the men in a pair of snug, wine-colored briefs that molded obscenely to his form.

Priest couldn't have been happier. "Holy shit, the new boy is packing!"

Erron was determined not to blush tonight. "That's six hundred there. The hand's not over yet. I call."

Everyone watched as he took his seat and picked up his cards. With a single hand, he fanned out his queen-high flush on the table to the approval of his opponents.

His confidence soared until Priest laid down a king-high flush in spades.

The room was an uproar of whistles, taunting groans, and laughter as Erron shook his head. It was unbelievable. Priest's cards were so mismatched, it made no sense how he'd gained a flush after tossing three cards. He didn't even have a set that one logically built a straight from. For all of his swagger at the moment, his winning hand was a fluke.

Laughing like the devil, Priest raked his winnings, including Erron's clothes, into his little corner with wide outstretched arms. James glared at the man.

"You'll get these back after I win." Priest blew Erron a taunting kiss.

"It's James's deal, bitch." Erron's bravado was just for show. With his meager pile of chips in front of him, Erron knew how easy getting dragged into a hand where he cashed in briefs would be. If he lost, he'd be up for grabs for whoever won the game, which in this case looked suspiciously like Priest.

It wasn't as if Priest was hard on the eyes, just the opposite. He was handsome, rugged, and fit, and given the man's bawdy attitude, Erron suspected the sex held the likelihood for a lot of fun. It would be easier if he weren't being so fucking arrogant. Priest was so sure he'd already won his night that Erron prayed to Lady Luck over and over for the man to lose.

James dealt the cards, keeping an ever-present eye on Priest. A tense silence filled the room as looks continued to shift to the undressed crew member at the table. Now that the chance of a loser was so close, the nature of wolves was coming forth. Cards glided to each player's position until everyone had the requisite five cards.

"Why do you keep reaching into your pocket after every deal?" James's eyes flashed alive in recognition as his voice rose. "Wait a minute! Barrus, Priest has a remote!"

"Sonofabitch!"

Priest's eyes went wide as Barrus launched from his seat and tackled him to the ground. Players stood and watched the tangle on the floor.

"Get your hand out of my pocket, fucker!" Priest screamed at Barrus as he held him down and produced a small device of the same design and metal as the playing-card holder. Pressing Priest against the floor, he handed the small item to James.

James turned over Priest's, Barrus's, and his own cards and pressed the button on the remote. The holographic surface redrew the images on Priest's cards into a winning hand. James looked positively pissed.

"I knew there's no way you'd break the odds that often. You're not that good a player, you shit."

"I just wanted to have a little fun with the new guy!"

James handed Erron back his clothes. "You could have just asked him out, asshole. Game's over. Everyone gets their money back, but Priest's share gets split amongst everyone else."

"You can't do that!"

"I just did. Barrus and I will walk you back to your quarters, Erron. From now on, you'll hand the remote over before we play again, or I'll have Barrus beat your ass."

Erron pulled on his pants with a smug smile as Barrus stood and came to his side, creating a wall between him and the others. Teddy and Carson walked over to Priest who was still lying on the floor. He shrank as Carson reached down and took a fistful of his collar.

"You do remember the house rules against cheating, Priest? I mean, since you find them so important." Carson's chuckle was downright sinful.

Priest's face went slack as Teddy and Carson passed a conspiratorial look between each other.

"Cheaters are at the mercy of the remaining players. Thanks, Priest. I was hoping to get laid tonight."

A gloss of perspiration broke out across Priest's forehead. "You don't really mean…"

"You were going to make Erron go through with it. Maybe you shouldn't have made the rules in the first place."

"Oh shit."

Carson pulled Priest to his feet but kept a firm grasp on the pilot. "C'mon, Teddy. We're gonna see if our host here can take two cocks at the same time."

Teddy's harsh squeeze of Priest's ass elicited a yelp. "Let's find out, shall we?"

Carson was already starting to unfasten his pants with his free hand.

At that moment, James spun Erron away and Barrus helped usher him out the door while Priest rambled, trying to convince the guys to go easy on him.

Erron whined on purpose. "Aw, man! I wanted to watch that!"

"As if Gamin won't have my hide for what almost happened anyways." James shook his head. "I can't believe I let you get caught up in that. I should have known better."

Erron rolled his eyes. "I'm hardly a child, James. The worst thing that could have happened was I finally get laid for the first time in months. Besides, you kept your mouth shut for an awfully long time."

The trio walked along the hall as a close-knit unit. Upon reaching the lift, Barrus reached from behind to the touchpad, and they entered the lift. Erron fought a slight wave of dizziness as the lift ascended, but it quickly passed.

"I should have, but if Barrus or I won, we'd both share, so the odds were in our favor."

Erron burst out laughing. "You're a fucking pig!"

"You handled yourself really well. You'll get asked to play cards again, for sure." Barrus stroked the back of Erron's head and neck. Erron wanted to purr at the contact, having almost forgotten what therapy a touch could be.

James grumbled low. "Especially once the talk about your package gets around."

"I'm glad that Priest didn't get the chance."

"We're both glad." A strange sort of relief colored James's voice and Barrus's as well. It piqued Erron's curiosity.

The lift stopped, and the trio stepped out onto Beta deck, but Erron halted. Questions needled his mind, and he refused to let them go unanswered for the second time that night.

He spun on his escorts and narrowed his eyes on each in turn. "What's that supposed to mean?"

"What was what supposed to mean?"

"Why are you both so glad Priest didn't get a chance?"

James looked stunned and Barrus uncomfortable. "Um, Erron...Barrus and I have been talking—"

"James and I really like you a lot—"

"We know you haven't been on board long—"

"We've really enjoyed your company—"

Erron stood listening to the continuing back and forth, confused by their constant interruption of one another. They rambled on, saying a lot but nothing at the same time. It was a little unsettling for both of these confident men to chat at him like nervous teenagers.

"Stop." Erron raised both hands to break the jabbering. "Get to the point. You're not making any sense."

"Oh God. This usually isn't so hard." James dug his fingers into his scalp with a frustrated grunt.

Barrus placed his large hand on James's shoulder. "Go ahead, babe. Say it. After the guys start talking about tonight, this will be a lot harder. The wolves will start to circle."

James nodded and took a deep breath as he straightened his posture. He reached up and placed a hand alongside Erron's face. The nervousness in James's expression was genuine.

"Erron, we know you've been through a lot the last few months. We're really sorry for what happened, but we're really happy that you're on board. We haven't gotten a chance to know you as well as we'd like, but we want to change that. Barrus and I have been talking since you arrived. From what we've seen, we think you're what we've been looking for and we'd like to find out if we're right." James paused for a moment, starting and stopping twice before the words came out. "We were wondering if we could date you. Officially."

Chapter Four

"YOU WANT TO date me? Both of you? At the same time?" Erron stood, gaping at James and Barrus.

In the sudden silence, only the engine's faint hum was heard in the hollow corridor. James, noticeably fidgeting, reached behind him. Without further prompt, Barrus linked their hands together.

James swallowed, marshaling his courage. "Yes, we do." Gone was the bravado Erron expected from the pair. Only an anxious anticipation was present as they awaited his response.

"How would that even work?" Erron's gaze drifted as he mulled the concept over. Splitting his attention between two lovers always sounded wrong when he imagined it. The idea was too close to cheating for his tastes. He'd pictured having sex with two men at once—what conscious man hadn't in his lifetime—but the idea of dating two men as a triad had never occurred to him.

Barrus sounded as uncertain as his husband. "We're not sure. We've played with others before—more than once—but never with anyone we planned on keeping."

Erron stood like a small, lost child until James separated from Barrus, reached forward, and took his hand. With a gentle tug, he led Erron close to the pair and settled him between them as Barrus took his other hand. He was close enough to bask in their body heat, but they were paying him a welcome respect by not touching him beyond holding his hands. The heat of their palms was a delicious sensation. How tempting to get lost in their offer—to throw away caution and give in to his attraction.

Erron frowned as he tried to wrap his brain around it. "I get the feeling this isn't just like rolling into bed with you two."

With a light brush of his fingertips, James tucked an errant lock of Erron's hair over his ear. "No. We're looking for something more substantial than that."

How wonderful that sounded. If only Toby hadn't said similar things to him once upon a time. If only Toby hadn't thrown him away, making all those words meaningless. Every night, Erron still heard the professions of love that ended with him being cast aside. Some nights he still cried. Months had passed and the wounds hadn't healed. He wasn't sure if he was willing to go through that again.

It wasn't fair. The honest touch of James's fingers was warm, strumming Erron's need for intimacy. He found aspects of both men to be worth exploring. But the reminders of the things he had walked away from kept creeping back. Trust was hard enough with one man. How much worse with two?

Erron crushed his eyes closed and lowered his head without releasing their hands. "I just don't know."

"It's okay, Erron." The bass in Barrus's voice sent miniature tremors down Erron's spine, meeting the gentle hand stroking his lower back. "We understand you've been through a lot. You've been hurt, and we realize you have to think about this. We know this kind of flies in the face of our reputation. James and I don't expect you to give us an answer tonight."

James sighed. "We honestly didn't plan on asking you tonight. The stuff that went on at the poker game made us jump ahead of schedule."

Erron opened his eyes as a subtle touch on his chin nudged his head upward, making him look into James's eyes. "We don't know if this is going to work either, but we think it will be worth it to try."

"And if you decide this isn't what you want, we'll understand and still want to be your good friends."

"That will not change." James's face glowed with a soft smile.

Erron let go of both their hands and wrapped his arms around James. "Thank you."

James returned the favor, and Barrus closed in from behind, wrapping them in his large arms. Only Gamin had made Erron this much at home since the disaster called Toby.

"Now, you need to get back to the kitchen and take care of those items for Gamin." Each man dropped a quick kiss along the side of Erron's head before they released him. James spun Erron around and swatted his rear, sending him off in the direction of the mess hall.

"We won't pressure you, Erron. If you decide to try things out, just come and find us."

Erron looked back at the pair as they walked the other way with lingering glances over their shoulders. As enticing an offer as it was, Erron was terrified. Why hadn't they just asked him to bed? Handling a noncommittal fusing of flesh to appease a temporary need for affection was far easier. But now it was complicated with the minefield of a relationship. Coming on board the *Santa Claus*, Erron had hoped for a fling here and there, as the need arose, without the risk of emotional attachments. Now, it appeared to be impossible.

He shook his head to clear his thoughts as he headed to the mess hall. Now was not the time to make a decision. Tomorrow was the time to consider it further once the shock had worn off.

The lights in the mess hall were at a minimum at this time of night, but for a sole light coming from the kitchen. As he wove between the rows of tables and chairs, a sound rang out of glass bouncing and rolling on the floor. His pulse quickened and his skin flushed. James and Barrus's offer might have scared him, but he wished they were there at the moment.

He edged in, passing the buffet counter as cold sweat rose on his back. Light spilled from the hinged double doors to the kitchen, and the sound of movement came from behind them. With a shaky hand, he creeped the door ajar at an impossibly slow pace, then peered through the narrow opening.

Gamin sat on the kitchen floor, his body swaying against the counter to his back. His lidded eyes appeared to be staring at nothing in particular. A tumbler lay on its side a number of meters away, and just outside of Gamin's reach was an empty liquor bottle.

"Gamin?" Erron's voice sounded louder in the quiet than it should have been. Gamin lolled his head in Erron's direction and fixed him with a vacant stare. Entering the room, Erron looked around. How long had Gamin been there?

"Stay here. I'll be right back." Erron hurried to the freezer and took care of the items Gamin had requested to be thawed. Why Gamin hadn't done it himself while he was there, Erron didn't know.

He came back to find Gamin exactly in the same place. Even growing up, he'd never seen the man drunk off his ass. Sighing, Erron collected the glass and empty bottle, hoping it hadn't all been drunk that night, but somehow, he knew better.

"Come on. Let's get you home."

Gamin only responded in growls and grunts as Erron grabbed his wrist and pulled him to his clumsy feet. Thank God, he was participating. If he fought or passed out, there was no way Erron had a chance of carrying him. Gamin was so much bigger and heavier than Erron. For a moment, he wondered if he should call James and Barrus for help but decided against it. He didn't want anyone to see Gamin like this. It was the least he could do for the man who had taught him to shave, among other things.

Erron helped support Gamin's unsteady steps as they worked their way back to the lift. Reaching Gamin's quarters was exhausting. More than once, Gamin stumbled, slamming Erron into the wall on their journey. Gamin didn't even seem to notice. It was a miracle that he never dropped to the floor or no one else witnessed it.

At the door, Erron planted his feet to keep upright as he tried to lift Gamin's hand to activate the DNA ID scan to open the door. With a childish groan, Gamin resisted the move, snatching his hand away, throwing his weight off center.

"Oh shit!" They were going to capsize. Erron reached out to steady them, his hand slamming into the door-lock panel. The lock disengaged and the door hissed open. Inside, the lights automatically came on at a low level. Why did that work?

There was no time to consider it. Gamin was starting to falter. Erron aimed their sloppy stumble at the bed, thankfully landing in the middle with a crashing bounce. It took a little work, but he managed to pry himself out from under Gamin's arm as the door closed behind them. Erron sat on the edge as Gamin settled and snuffled face-first into the mattress.

Erron took a quick look around. The room was identical to his own, but Gamin's space was tidier. Only a few items were lying about, so the miniature, flat metal disc on the nightstand caught his notice, even in the low light. So many years had passed without Gamin, he wondered if this contained some of those missing events. Pressing a single finger to the surface, its small lens flared and a holographic picture appeared.

The likeness of a handsome man—who seemed a little older than Erron—hovered over the device. The tagline under the image simply said "Niven." With a swipe of his finger, Erron paged through a number of photos of the same man in various places on the ship. He was always smiling with those deep chocolate eyes, the pure happiness in his grin somehow intimate. Who was Niven? Someone special, perhaps? With the missing period of years between Gamin and Erron's lives, there were still many questions he wanted to ask. Even so, he knew he shouldn't be looking at these images. Guilt seeped into his chest at the invasion of privacy. Erron switched off the holo.

Erron peeked back to Gamin. He hadn't moved and hadn't seen anything, but it didn't make Erron feel any better. It was time to go.

"Good night, Gamin." Erron leaned over and placed a feathery kiss along Gamin's temple. His reward was to be enveloped by a beefy arm and dragged down onto the bed. Like a child with a security blanket, Gamin pulled Erron into his sleeping body. Every time he tried to squirm free, Gamin tightened his grip. Attempts to wake Gamin up were equally futile. Dwarfed by the older, larger man, there was no way he was getting out from the anaconda grip. Erron resigned himself to his fate.

He supposed there were worse fates. Surrounded by Gamin, Erron's exhaustion over the night's events took its toll. The full body contact was so inviting, like being pressed against the most comfortable, warm body pillow he'd ever known. Staying the night wasn't a chore. He'd worry about the following morning later.

"Mrs. Claus. Wake-up call for me at 05:00 hours at this location. Lights out."

Mrs. Claus's synthetic voice chimed back as the room went dark. "Your wake-up call has been programmed. Good night, Mr. Murfin."

Erron fell asleep, completely at ease.

IT WAS THE most magnificent dream. A stranger pinned Erron facedown to the mattress. He didn't know who it was, but he found himself relishing the delicious weight dominating him. Wet bites, hard enough to sting but not to bruise, chewed along his neck and shoulder line accompanied by a series of throaty growls. Heavy insistent prodding of an obvious erection demanded entrance to his backside. The rhythmic pressure kneaded his own turgid member into the mattress below. One thrust after another was driving him to boil over. Erron had almost forgotten how good it was to be beneath another man.

He was so close. Erron felt the cock behind him grow larger and harder. They would both reach a sweaty end in short order.

"Good morning, Mr. Murfin. It is now 05:00 hours."

Erron startled awake as the room's light panels automatically turned on to their lowest setting. The weight of the stranger was still upon him and so was the steel bar of flesh pressed into the cleft of his ass. A growling voice confused him further.

"What the fuck?"

With a sudden scramble, the weight lifted. Looking over his shoulder, Erron found a pale and rumpled Gamin. His weary eyes were wide in shock, paired with an unmistakable visage of terror. Gamin's baffled stare scanned between the room, Erron, and himself. Pulling a pillow from the bed, Gamin covered his swollen groin. Both men were still completely clothed, but it did nothing to dampen the growing taste of shame in the room.

"Why are you in my room?" Gamin's eyes were wild as he kept shifting away from Erron, keeping the pillow over himself, a chaste shield.

"I found you all fucked up in the kitchen. I helped you back here and you pulled me into bed. I couldn't get out, so I stayed the night."

The horror in Gamin's expression made Erron avert his eyes.

"It's no big deal."

Gamin said nothing. Erron waited for a response to no avail. The dense silence ate at him, its jagged disquiet cutting deep. Sitting upright, Erron pulled his knees to his chest, making himself tiny and self-conscious as he wrapped his arms around his legs. Gamin faced away on the bed's edge, cradling his head in his large hands.

What was he supposed to do now? Technically, nothing happened, but in a way, it did. Given Gamin's reaction, it was a bad, horrible thing—rotten. The tight crease forming between Erron's brows deepened into a chasm. Frustrated, Erron ran his hands through his hair, tugging at the jade locks.

"Get up and get to work." Gamin stood, walked to his clothing storage, and pulled out a fresh set of clothes. With his back turned, he made a deliberate effort not to look at Erron.

Too aware of the sickening heat filling him, Erron climbed off the bed and crept to the door. He glanced back at Gamin, who continued to pay him no attention whatsoever. As the door slid shut behind him, Erron took a deep breath and held it, holding back the tears trying to fall as he shuffled back to his own quarters.

IT WAS THE first day cooking hadn't made Erron happy. Prepping breakfast was an exercise in awkward silence. The only sounds in the kitchen were the knives working the cutting board and the sizzle of food on the grill. Gamin avoided his eyes and neither man ate before they dug into their work. Erron's appetite had long since been lost.

For the first time since he'd come on board, Erron wore the bulkiest shirt and pants he owned. It made him too warm in the heat of the galley, but the sight of Gamin's revulsion at the prospect of waking up in bed together replayed over and over in Erron's head. He hadn't felt so unwanted or unattractive since the day Toby ended their relationship.

Erron served the men alone when meal service began. Gamin continued to work in the back, probably to nurse his hangover into some semblance of health. The friendly dialogue with the crew did little to reverse his isolation. He forced himself to smile through the service.

"Morning, Erron."

"Morning, James. Morning, Barrus."

In their usual fashion, James and Barrus arrived together. Smiling and pleasant, they chose from the menu, showing a genuine excitement over the breakfast selection. Erron served up hearty portions to both, having learned their appetites in the few short weeks since coming on board.

Barrus looked around the mess hall. "I'm impressed that Gamin leaves you alone up here."

It was intended to be a compliment—Erron knew that—but the memory of waking up and being dismissed by Gamin seared him and stuck its tines into his chest.

Erron inhaled to swallow down the rejection. "Yeah. He's in the back."

"Are you all right?" James looked genuinely concerned.

"I'm fine. Why do you ask?"

Barrus frowned as he assessed Erron closer. "You seem a little off today. Anything we can do?"

"No, I'm fine. I just didn't sleep well last night." Of course, that wasn't true. Erron had rarely slept so well. Sleeping with Gamin had been easier than it should have been. It was the wake-up requiring a reboot.

James's voice softened and his expression flattened. "Oh."

"Not because of you two." Erron shook his head. "I have my own issues to sort out."

"You sure?" James didn't look convinced. Erron was glad to see them both but didn't want to deal with their offer right then. His mind was too mired in the state of his relationship with Gamin. Straightening his posture, he put on his best smile for both their benefits.

"Yes. Go eat. I didn't do all this work to have it go to waste. I'll talk to you both soon."

The sadness in James's face dissipated. "All right. Com us if you need anything."

Erron nodded. "I will."

With a gentle nudge, Barrus directed James to follow him to their usual seats. Erron was amazed at how, even sitting across from each other, they gravitated to one another. There was an undeniable closeness between them. And they wanted him to be a part of it.

"Morning, Erron."

"Hey, Carson. Nice to see you again, Priest."

Carson had a grip on Priest's collar. Sheepish and head down, he allowed himself to be led along the food line.

"Priest has something he wanted to say to you."

"Oh really?"

When Priest stayed silent, Carson grabbed the lobe of the pilot's ear and pinched.

"Ow! Okay! Okay!" Priest squirmed away from Carson, rubbing his ear. "I'm sorry about the game last night. I shouldn't have cheated you like that."

"It's all right. I didn't get fucked over in the end, so I'm not sore about it. Oh, sorry. Is that a tender subject?"

Carson snorted, and Priest shot him a dirty look. Erron wondered if it had anything to do with how Priest was walking a bit stiff. When he moved just right, a subtle wince appeared. The payback activity with Carson and Teddy must have been vigorous. Priest almost sounded penitent as he continued.

"Erron, I was wondering... You got any plans tonight?" His contrite tone became decidedly bawdy. "I might be able to find a way to make it up to you. We don't need the cards to have a good time."

Erron stood there unable to respond. Looking offended at Priest's suggestion, Carson swatted him hard on the ass. Priest yelped loud enough to stop conversations through the whole room. A chorus of knowing snickers and laughter drifted amongst the crew. Priest's face flamed as he collected his food and moved on without another word.

Eventually, the morning meal schedule came to a close. Erron wiped his brow as he collected the remnants from the buffet so they could start prepping for the lunch service. With a towel over his shoulder, he set the empty tray on the counter and nearly jumped when Gamin's heavy hand palmed his shoulder.

"Erron, sit down."

Slumping into a seat at one of the prep tables, Erron threw his towel down and absentmindedly wiped the surface in small circles. Only one meal down, and he was exhausted. This was going to be a difficult day. He was so distracted, he barely registered the plate of food Gamin set before him. Another chair scraped along the floor, and Gamin sat down next to Erron with a plate of his own.

"I'm really sorry about last night." Gamin took a reluctant bite of his own sandwich.

Erron picked at his sandwich and tore a corner off the fresh bread. He chewed the offering as he spoke low. "Yeah, well, the night was no picnic, but I'll live. The morning was way worse." He picked up his food and took a deep bite. Like with everything Gamin made, it was full of flavor, but Erron found no enjoyment in it.

"I'm sorry, Erron. I handled that so badly."

Erron shrugged and lowered his head in an attempt to hide his eyes with his jade-colored bangs. "It's okay. I can understand how I'm not the man you wanted to wake up to."

"That's not it at all." Gamin nearly choked as he swallowed. "It's just been a long time since anyone's been in my bed."

Erron looked from the corner of his eye as sadness crept into Gamin's face. He stopped eating, lost in whatever memories he saw through his vacant eyes.

"Was Niven the last one?"

If Gamin looked sad before, now he was completely stricken. Grief etched his face as his features fell. His unfocused eyes became glassy and his jaw quivered. Abruptly, he stood, picked up his plate, and dumped it, food and all, into the recycler.

"I need to start lunch. Eat up and let's get started." The words were thick and halting.

Erron's shoulders fell as he stared back at his own lunch. Now he definitely didn't have an appetite.

THE DOOR TO Erron's quarters slid open at the touch of his hand. Freshly showered and soul weary, he shuffled into the room. Baggy clothes still stained from work unceremoniously hit the floor one slow piece at a time. After work was complete, Erron had headed straight to the showers without bothering to change clothes.

Silence and unspoken sadness had colored Gamin's mood for the rest of the day. The morning was awkward enough, yet once again, Erron discovered his talent for poor timing. Why did Niven's name elicit such sorrow? The pain radiating off Gamin all day was suffocating. Erron wanted to know, to talk to Gamin and make things right between them, but the fear he'd more likely make the situation worse kept him quiet. It was difficult to walk away at the end of the evening, but Gamin left the kitchen with barely a word.

Perhaps it was best to leave it alone. If Gamin wanted him to know, Gamin had all the time in the cluster to share. If only he could get the image of those handsome brown eyes out of his mind. He wished he'd never touched the holo. Now it was too late to take back.

He pulled a fresh pair of shorts over his thighs, the skin still lightly seared from his shower. Erron had stood under the spray, turned up as hot as the system allowed, until his skin screamed and he had to stop. It hadn't granted him atonement.

He scrubbed a towel through his hair as Mrs. Claus broke the quiet. "A private transmission coming through Subspace Link for you, Mr. Murfin."

Erron's brow rose in confusion. Who the fuck knew he was on board? Erron hadn't received a com since arriving on board. A flashing icon on the monitor mounted to the wall over his desk taunted his curiosity. Who bothered to contact him? Everyone he knew was either on the ship, dead, or had walked out on him. Wary but interested, Erron sat and activated the link.

As soon as he saw the grinning man on the screen, he wished he'd ignored it.

"Nice! All wet and shirtless. You'd think you knew I was calling."

Erron didn't find his natural playfulness funny in the least. "Why are you calling me, Toby?"

The handsome man raised his hands in defense as if Erron could actually reach him through the screen. If only that were possible. The waves of his golden hair were disheveled, and he wore a sleeveless undershirt in the dim lighting of what looked like a home office. Coarse stubble graced his firm jawline, making Erron remember the scrub of it on his skin.

"I went through a lot of effort to find you, Erron. I wanted to talk to you."

Memories of rejection simmered inside Erron's chest. At the same time, he found himself impressed by the effort, but not for long. A mix of pain and attraction waged war as he studied the man who had known him better than anyone else. The stress of his trouble with Gamin had left him unprepared for a new wave of emotion. Erron wrapped his arms around his chest, but not to fight off the cold.

"You found me. Talk."

Toby's shoulders sank. "Don't be like that, Erron."

"Don't be like what? You can't believe I'd be excited to see you or even want to talk to you after what you did to me."

"You haven't disconnected me, either."

Erron paused. His pulse quickened as he studied Toby's lips. The strong, bare arms that had held him down so many nights beckoned to him.

"I wanted to see how you were, Erron. You look good." A slight smile formed on Toby's face. "I like that you kept the green hair."

"After you dumped me and fired me, I didn't have the currency for the treatment to make it grow natural again."

The smile faded. "I'm sorry, Erron. It wasn't supposed to be like that. I tried to talk to my dad, but he wouldn't listen. He threatened to cut me off if I didn't go along."

"Oh, well congratulations. You saved yourself."

"Please, Erron. You know I'm not as strong as you. I never was."

"You don't have to be strong. Someone always takes care of you." Erron turned his attention to a blank spot on the floor. "Some of us aren't so lucky."

The near imperceptible hum of the atmospherics only amplified the heat of betrayal. Toby's charming demeanor failed to extinguish the charring burn still lingering inside Erron. Why did Toby have to call and open up the wounds he wanted to walk away from after all this time?

"I want you back."

Erron's head snapped to Toby. "Excuse me?"

"I miss you, Erron. I was hoping the next time you docked in Alpha Centauri you might come to see me."

"You're not getting married?" He hadn't wanted to sound like he pined for Toby, for the good memories he missed, but the soft hopeful note in Erron's voice seeped out.

Toby's gaze shifted away. "I kind of have to. It wouldn't be right at this point not to."

"She's pregnant, isn't she?"

Toby said nothing as he looked everywhere but at Erron.

"For fuck's sake, Toby! You can't be serious!" Erron shook his head in disbelief.

"I can make it good for us."

"Planning to set me up in a nice apartment so I can be around whenever you need a fix away from your wife and kids?"

"You're the one I really want."

Erron's voice quivered. "Were you planning on leaving me money on the nightstand on your way out the door?"

"It won't be like that. I love you, Erron."

"No, you don't." He took a deep breath and swallowed hard. "You only love one person in the whole cluster—yourself. I can't believe it's taken me this long to realize it."

"Don't talk like that."

Erron's eyes swelled and his words became louder. "It makes me sick to think I loved you so much. You used to tell me how much you loved me too. But you would have said anything to get me into your bed. And you did. And I believed it."

"Keep your voice down!"

"*You fucking bastard!*" Erron's volume was completely unrestrained. "*She's in the house, isn't she? You were with her earlier, weren't you? And now you're calling me to get me back on the side?*"

The lack of response and the guilt on Toby's face confirmed it. In utter disgust, Erron slammed his hand on the disconnect icon. The disappearance of Toby's image did nothing to calm the disquiet broiling in his chest. Was it really possible to be enraged, ashamed, and stupid at the same time?

Erron stood, his shoulders shaking as he scrubbed his face with his hands. It had been months since he'd laid eyes on Toby, let alone spoken to him. Why did this have to be so painful?

He knew why. All those years had added up to giving his heart to a selfish, opportunistic man, and Erron had blinded himself to his severe character flaws. *That's what you get when you're so desperate to be loved after the losses in your life, you're willing to believe anything.* The loved ones he'd seen suffer during the civil war, his mother and so many friends, had left a deep longing inside Erron. Toby seemed like the perfect solution. Perhaps in his need, he had imagined him into the role, oblivious of the reality.

When Toby talked about wanting to see him, for a moment a tiny voice had cried out for a second chance, a way to make things right. Erron should have known better. Toby was irredeemable, incapable of making an honest, suitable mate to anyone. Why did it still hurt? Why did he ache over shutting down the chat? How sad a human being did he have to be to allow that kind of man into his life, let alone his bed?

Coupling the shame with the horrific night and day with Gamin, Erron felt especially needy. It wasn't fair. He believed he was a good person. Why didn't someone else see it? After picking out a fresh shirt, he covered himself. Erron couldn't bring himself to stay undressed. Only confident attractive men did such things.

Mrs. Claus chimed in again. "A private transmission coming through Subspace Link for you, Mr. Murfin." The icon on his monitor flashed, the Link address the same as before. Toby was trying to call him back.

"Mrs. Claus, block coms from that frequency and user. Unless it's a death notice."

"Block established, Mr. Murfin."

Erron ran an unsteady hand over his welling eyes. He found his quarters uninviting and claustrophobic. He slipped on a pair of shoes, touched the control pad, and was out the door.

Fortunately, no one was about. Erron's nerves were a rapid simmer and he simply didn't want to see anyone. The faint hum of the ship's engines usually lulled him to sleep at night, but now the white noise was drowned out by his ragged breathing. It wasn't long before he found himself in front of another door identical to his.

Erron rolled his fingers in and out of his fist and his bleary eyes burned a hole into the unyielding metal. He reached out and stopped himself several times before he finally touched the chime control. The door hissed open like the rest on the ship.

"Erron?" James stood in the doorway in a simple pair of lounging pants, his trim muscles on display. The smile on his face evaporated with one quick look at Erron's fractured demeanor. "What's wrong?"

Words refused to form as the tremors increased and the tears overflowed Erron's eyes. It took nothing for James to reach forward and gently pull Erron into his arms. He buried himself into the contact because he was too overwrought to speak aloud.

Barrus appeared from deeper in the room and surrounded the pair. "Erron, are you all right?"

"It went so wrong. I just... Gamin... Toby... I didn't know where else to go." The reply came out in choked syllables. He was on the verge of full-out sobs. The events of the last twenty-four-hour cycle had been too much. Erron had no idea of how to cope with it. The emotional garbage he thought was disposed of had resurfaced in a matter of minutes, brand-new and festering.

The arms surrounding him were emotional armor as they drew him closer. Barrus stroked the back of Erron's head and placed a kiss along his temple. Two pairs of hands and two pairs of lips worked with platonic caresses to soothe him.

"Shh…it's all right. Don't worry, Erron. We'll take care of you."

Erron pressed into the warmth as someone reached back and closed the door behind them.

Chapter Five

ERRON WOKE EARLY as he always did. This time, however, he was still dressed and nestled between the slumbering forms of James and Barrus. It was dark in their shared quarters. A soft glow from the monitor's time code bathed the room with just enough illumination to hide the inky blackness of space. Erron's face was comfortable on James's shoulder with one arm holding him close enough to scent the firm chest dusted with blond hair. Barrus's large body pressed against his back, his heavy arm and leg draped over Erron. Cocooned between them, he was shielded from the outside world. All three men were in contact of one sort or another. A soft sigh drifted out of Erron, the touches felt so right. The men surrounding him were warm and chased away the swamping loneliness from the previous night.

A tinge of embarrassment heated his face as he recalled how long they'd had to hold him until the crying subsided. They laid him to bed and, between them, covered his body with soothing hugs and caring caresses. Erron had pressed into the heat of loving arms and hands, never realizing how much he'd needed and craved it. How easy it would have been to take advantage of him under the circumstances.

But they had been perfect gentlemen. The reputation following James and Barrus as voracious satyrs missed the truth of their softer sides. Both men were capable of tender, nurturing care, without requiring payment for services rendered.

The soft breath of Barrus's sleep warmed the nape of Erron's neck as he studied James. Even in the minimal light, the man's strong jawline was obvious. Beautiful where Barrus was rugged, James was almost angelic as he slept. Erron kept to himself how attractive he thought both men were. In a silent thanks, he placed a soft kiss on James's chest and then on Barrus's arm curled around his shoulder and torso.

Both men's embrace tightened at the gesture. Erron closed his eyes in rapture. Soft fingertips brushed his hairline.

"How are you doing?" James's whisper went almost unheard. "Feeling better?"

Erron nodded and opened his eyes. There was James, drowsy yet paying close attention. Sliding his hand along James's neck, Erron shifted forward to brush a soft kiss along his lips.

"You don't have to do that."

"I know." Once again, Erron closed the gap between them. When Erron licked at James's lips, any resistance he'd shown evaporated. With a soft groan, James gave back in kind, fusing their mouths together. James tasted his mouth with unrestrained energy as their tongues slid along each other. Barrus's arms constricted and a series of heavy wet kisses and bites trailed along the path of Erron's neck and shoulders.

It was easy to lose track of whose kneading hands were whose as all three men explored each other. Somehow, everyone's clothes stripped away amidst the growing frenzy. Did he really stop kissing James long enough to remove his shirt? Cupping Erron's face with his free hand, James pulled back, his darkened eyes tracing the pout of Erron's lips. Gently, he turned Erron's head, nodding toward Barrus. Once he understood the meaning, Erron rolled over to entwine himself chest to chest in Barrus's arms.

"Lights. Lowest setting." Barrus growled in the dark. The light panels came to life, casting a sultry glow matching the room's attitude. "I want to see us."

Barrus's kiss was more fierce and demanding than James's. Erron lost himself as Barrus held him still, his large hands threaded into Erron's hair as he plundered his mouth. Heated bites stung Erron's lips before a commanding tongue chased his own. Having changed places, James pressed into Erron's back, shamelessly grinding his skin and body against him. A rigid column of flesh urged forward between his buttocks. It teased at Erron's opening, not trying to enter, simply tickling the sensitive ring.

Erron's breath came in needy huffs, his sense of self becoming lost within the lusty haze. With a careful fistful of Erron's hair, Barrus pulled him back. His heated stare gave away more than simple arousal.

Glints of amber lit Barrus's eyes. "You are so beautiful. We both love how your hair matches the color of your eyes."

James whispered into Erron's ear, "We both want you. Can I? Can we?"

Erron nodded through his quickened breath. His voice had lost its will to function.

Barrus pulled Erron closer still, his dense musculature and thick body hair sending rushes through Erron's flesh. Chewing along Erron's neck, Barrus thrust his hips against him, sliding both their cocks along one another. After the familiar noise of storage doors opening behind him, James's slippery fingers began the slow, deliberate process of entry. One finger, then two worked their way inside, stretching him, until Erron rocked back, silently begging for more. James's cock was thick, and burned in all the right ways. Pinned between the pair, Erron was simply along for the ride. Reaching back for James's head with one hand, he gripped Barrus with the other to pull them closer as he reveled in being the center of the rutting. Each thrust forced him harder against Barrus, eliciting a moan with each stroke.

Words were lost. Only guttural noises filled the room for long, heated minutes.

James's grip went from firm to bruising. "I...I can't hold out any longer, Erron. Oh fuck." Losing the cadence of his stroke, James spilled inside Erron with a series of primal grunts and gasps. He extracted himself with care, continuing to lay kisses along Erron's shoulder and neck, then met with Barrus's hungry mouth as he rolled Erron on his back. James's arm served as a makeshift pillow as Barrus climbed between Erron's legs.

Barrus planted a deep kiss on James, then on Erron in turn as he raised Erron's legs. With the slightest shift of his hips, the security officer's heated member nudged at the entrance. Erron was still slick with James's release, so Barrus's engorged cock slid inside with a single push. Erron praised the entry from deep within, wrapping his legs around the big man's waist and using his heels to spur him deeper.

With one arm wrapped around James lying beside him and one around the shoulder and neck of Barrus, Erron rolled his hips, urging Barrus to give him the punishing fuck he desperately wanted.

"Harder!" It was the only coherent word Erron had uttered since it began. Barrus did not disappoint as he increased his speed and intensity. Erron's need was spiraling out of control. How long had it been since he'd submitted beneath another man?

James wet his palm and grabbed Erron's rigid shaft. "That's it, baby. I want to make that fat cock shoot while he fucks you out of your mind."

Erron gasped and arched his back as he was stroked from inside and out. Tightening his arm around Erron, James alternated hard kisses between each of his partners. His grip firmed as he corkscrewed Erron's dripping shaft. The slick friction built a charge through Erron's body, threatening to wring out a screaming end.

It didn't take long. Erron bucked and shouted as he released in forceful streaks, lining his chest and coating James's hand. The clenching spasms of his tunnel made Barrus's face twist in climax.

"Oh shit, Erron! Take it!" With one, two, three brutal thrusts, Barrus roared and emptied himself, his chest heaving in erratic pants.

Barrus collapsed on top of Erron, who found himself still receiving kisses and touches, the pulses from both men transmitting through the contact. Bit by bit, the drumming heartbeats calmed as everyone's breathing leveled out. Sticky and sated, Erron floated in bliss as the three of them lounged in a lazy pile.

"Good morning." Did Erron just giggle?

Barrus rolled to look at the monitor's time stamp. "It is not morning. It's still the night before."

"Some of us have to get up early and cook for you rowdy lot." Erron laughed. "You better start getting used to it."

A dawning light appeared in James's face. "You mean it? This was more than a one-off?" He tried to hide his excitement but was failing.

"I think so. I definitely want to see how it works. I was in a threesome one night a long time ago. My ex talked me into it. It was really disconnected, and I didn't know who to pay attention to. I got a little jealous when he seemed to enjoy the other guy too much. In the end, I didn't really enjoy it. That's not what's happening here."

James leaned forward and touched a soft kiss to Erron's mouth. "Give us an honest chance, Erron. This isn't about us taking turns, or some kind of boredom between me and Barrus. We both want you as much as we want each other. We want this to be good for *all* of us."

Barrus squeezed the pair in his mighty arms and lavished happy kisses on both. Bubbling yet quiet laughter filled the room. Where had Erron found the luck that these two handsome men had chosen him? He sensed open intentions with no pretense or hidden agendas. The intimacy of the three of them lying in bed was something Erron missed.

"Now that that decision is settled..." James tipped Erron's chin up, forcing him to meet his eyes. "Do you want to tell us what happened last night?"

Erron's brow flattened and he tried to look away, but surrounded by the men as he was, he found there was nowhere to hide. "I had a really upsetting com from my ex. He tracked me down after almost five months."

"I can understand that. He was the reason you found the *Santa Claus*, right?" Barrus gently stroked the locks from Erron's forehead.

"Yeah. But the whole thing just iced the cake. The whole day had been a big mess."

Barrus's hand stilled. "What do you mean?"

Erron hesitated. As much as he wanted to be completely honest with both of them, a little voice told him to edit his thoughts. This might not be the best time to mention how he'd spent the night with Gamin and woke up with the sleeping man humping him. His new lovers, if that's what he should call them, didn't need that detail. Not yet. If ever.

"Gamin and I had a stupid, ugly disagreement first thing in the morning. It looked like we were getting over it, but I fucked it up. It was awful."

"What was the argument over?"

"It doesn't really matter."

"How did it go to hell after?"

"We were in the middle of apologizing, and I asked him about Niven. Whoever he is. Gamin got really upset and then didn't talk to me for the rest of the day."

A look flashed between James and Barrus.

"What?"

James shook his head. "It's nothing."

"What do you mean? Who's Niven?"

"Gamin didn't tell you?" Barrus sounded hesitant to speak.

"No."

"Then it's really not our place to tell you about it."

Erron opened his mouth to speak, but James cut him off with a whisper.

"Seriously, Erron. Please don't ask." His voice echoed the sad look in his eyes as he took his turn stroking the hair along Erron's forehead.

While James wasn't being rude or demanding, his stance was rigid. Erron knew continuing at this point was fruitless, if not outright rude. The mere mention of Niven's name had changed the room's tone and he couldn't pin down what he was reading from them. He knew he'd have to find another avenue.

"It doesn't matter now. But as much as I'd love to stay in bed for many more hours soaking up the lusty attention of you two, I need to get a shower and get to work. I'm pretty sure you two have worked up a good appetite for breakfast."

Barrus bit at Erron's shoulder with a playful growl. "Then you better get up before I show you what kind of appetite I have in the morning and take a bite out of that nice ass."

Erron bounced out of bed as Barrus swiped at his bare backside, laughing along as he searched the room for where his clothing may have landed. His shirt was in one corner and his shorts in the complete opposite direction. It was torture to keep from peeking at the bed. Another good look at the inviting pair sprawled over the covers and he might end up tempted to be late to work for a change. To keep the thoughts of more sex at bay, he quickly covered himself. He had yet to go completely soft, and a new erection would make him a fresh target. The whole time he felt dual appreciative stares lingering over his skin.

THE BREAKFAST SERVICE ended and the temperature between Erron and Gamin was still unexpectedly cool. Little had been said between them and Erron was hesitant to speak first after ruining things before by asking about Niven. He wanted to know more but didn't dare. Another method would have to be found to answer his questions. How did the mention of one man's name bring such sadness to anyone? Whoever Niven was to Gamin, Erron felt compelled to understand. It was obviously something big if James and Barrus were staying quiet as well.

The lunch and supper services weren't much better. Gamin spoke only when necessary and had Erron serving whenever possible, keeping him out of the kitchen during meal times. The frustration was on the edge of a boil and threatened to scald. Erron wasn't sure what to do. This had to blow over soon, didn't it?

Erron cleaned up the buffet counter after the last hour of the meal service expired. He shut down the warming elements and removed the serving pans to be placed in the sanitizer. Fitting everything neatly into the machine, Erron started the cleaning cycle. It was one of the last items on the list before closing up the kitchen for the night—after another stressful day.

When Gamin approached him, Erron stiffened in reflex.

"Erron." Gamin motioned to the table. "Sit down. Please."

This moment seemed all too familiar. What new ghastliness would they unearth this time? Taking a seat, Erron slumped his shoulders. The last two days' events in the kitchen had worn him down. Gamin walked around him, but Erron refused to meet his glance or speak a word. Too many mistakes had been made between them and Erron didn't want to risk damaging their friendship further. They'd only been reunited for a short time. So intent on being quiet, Erron almost didn't notice the plate Gamin slid in front of him.

"This is for you. I'm sorry about everything."

Erron looked down at the elaborate personal-sized cake in front of him. A perfect circle fifteen centimeters across and fifteen centimeters tall, the scent of coffee, chocolate, and cinnamon graced his senses. The icing was a mirror-smooth glaze in delicate white and silky brown marbling. A single sugar-glass rose adorned the top, perfectly centered. It was almost too beautiful to eat.

"It's not my birthday. Mom always made one of these for me for my birthday."

Gamin nudged Erron's shoulder with the back of his hand. "Who do you think taught her to make it? It was always meant for special occasions. Three layers of cake: chocolate, chocolate cheesecake, and chocolate with cinnamon ganache between them. Cream cheese, vanilla, and chocolate swirl glazing. You always loved chocolate. It took me all day to make that without you finding out. It was hard keeping you up front serving to give me the chance. I decided it was okay not to wait for your birthday."

Erron's eyes welled at the gift. He patted the stool next to him and Gamin shared the table. He looked expectantly at Erron, obviously nervous and waiting for a response. With a sheepish smile, he looked Gamin directly in the eye.

"Will you share it with me?"

Gamin's relieved grin lit up the room. "I'd be delighted."

After retrieving an additional utensil, Gamin sliced out a careful wedge, exposing the delicious layers. Erron's mouth watered at the sight. His fork bit into the cake and the taste was better than he'd ever remembered. Pleasure overloaded his mouth and Erron closed his eyes as he moaned at the memory and the flavor. When he opened them again, he caught the sly grin on Gamin's face, making him blush all the way to his ears.

"I'll take that noise as approval." Gamin chuckled as he took a bite of his own.

"This is incredible." Erron purred as another large bite disappeared into his mouth. The silky chocolate left its delicate trace behind, allowing him to savor it between samples.

Gamin turned his head away slightly. "It was the least I could do. You didn't deserve the way I reacted that morning. Or the day after."

For long minutes, both men shared the peace offering with the sounds of laughing and small grunts of chocolate satisfaction. Nothing was spoken of the underlying issue, but at this point, right then, it didn't matter. Erron had Gamin back, the Gamin that loved his company and made him belong on board. Bite after bite, the dessert dwindled, often between giggles as they occasionally clashed forks over a particularly enticing morsel.

"Erron." Gamin's stilted voice belied the calm smile on his face. "There's something I wanted to ask you for a while."

"Now that's the smile I like to see on you."

Both men turned to find Barrus standing in the kitchen doorway.

"Barrus. What brings you here?" Gamin asked.

"Just thought I'd check to see if Erron was free. James and I were going to watch a vid and have a nightcap. Interested?"

Gamin sounded a touch wary, a touch confused. "That sounds a lot like a date."

Erron hedged a bit, unsure of Gamin's opinion. "Date is the right word." While the chef's smile was gone, he didn't appear upset either. His neutral expression was unreadable.

"When did this come about?"

Erron shrugged. "Officially, this morning."

"Or last night depending on how you read the clock." Barrus sniggered.

"Shut up!" Erron cocked a brow at Barrus in exasperation. He slowly turned back to Gamin. "I never got the chance to tell you."

"It's not your fault. Since this dessert is finished, why don't you put away the last stock in the back pantry so we can get you out of here." Gamin stood and patted Erron's shoulder. The familial contact put Erron at ease. For some reason, he was leery of telling Gamin about his new relationship.

"Thanks, Gamin. By the way, what did you want to ask me?"

Gamin shook his head. "It wasn't important. Now finish up so you can go have some fun."

"This won't take long, Barrus. I'll meet you and James after I take a quick shower."

"Sounds good. You can find us in the rec room for the vid."

Erron jumped up and strode through the doors into the rear pantry. He busied himself with placing the various bulk crates back into their respective locations. The cake ingredients containers were out of the pantry. He imagined Gamin pulling them out in a hurry and leaving them behind while trying to keep the process secret.

The last crate went to the top shelf and Erron had to steady himself from a head rush as he climbed the stepladder. It passed as quickly as it came. When was that going to stop happening? He stepped off the ladder and looked around at the tidy space. The task went quicker than expected.

He untied his apron and headed back into the kitchen area. Voices trying to be quiet were heard as he opened the door. Gamin was standing uncomfortably close to Barrus, jabbing his finger into the security guard's chest. They hadn't noticed him, so he stood back out of sight.

"Better treat him right. If I find out you two fuck that boy over, you won't be able to say the words 'food poisoning' faster than you'll hit the deck. That's assuming I don't beat your asses first."

"We'd never do that to him." Barrus's hands were raised in quiet defense. "If all we wanted was sex, we wouldn't go to this much effort to get to know him."

"For your sakes, you'd better be right about that. Now get out of here. Erron will find you soon enough." Gamin stood his ground as Barrus slowly backed off and left the room. Undisguised hostility radiated from Gamin. The chef was breathing hard and furious. He jerked open a nearby wall storage and retrieved a bottle of liquor. With a firm grip on the neck, he stormed out of the kitchen.

Erron stood perfectly still in complete confusion. What the fuck was that about?

"HAPPY ANNIVERSARY," ERRON whispered.

Had it really been a month already? Erron left an imperceptible kiss on each of James's and Barrus's slumbering forms. James's toned body curled around him while Barrus's large physique somehow surrounded and sheltered the two of them. How Erron managed to extricate himself from the body pile unnoticed was nothing short of miraculous. As quietly as possible he pulled on his clothes. The work shift was not far away. Once he was dressed, he glanced back over to his lovers still soundly asleep.

A wistful smile graced Erron's lips. Lovers. Waking up daily with a pair of extremely tactile men was something he never thought himself capable of. The insecurities nagging him since Toby had walked out on him were muted these days. It was the closest to happy Erron remembered being since even before Toby.

Erron crept over to the desk monitor and activated the screen. Wincing at the sudden brightness, he looked over his shoulder. Neither James nor Barrus registered any notice of the glow. Both appeared to be sleeping soundly. Once sure, he pulled up the ship's roster, past and present. There, in cyber green text, was what he was looking for, but not completely.

NIVEN ANDERS—SECURITY [FILE LOCKED—ACCESS DENIED]

Staring in frustration at the illuminated text, he ground his teeth as he hit another wall. This was no more information than what he'd found before. Using Barrus's terminal, he had hoped to get past the security clearance. A security officer locked out? Why? There wasn't even an option for a password to unlock the file.

Erron was worried. As happy as he had recently been, there was one thing marring the calm. In the last month, Gamin's behavior had deteriorated, and he was sure whatever silence surrounded Niven sat at the heart of it. Why wasn't anyone willing to discuss Niven with him? What were they trying to hide? With his work schedule, Erron hadn't had the chance to get to know anyone else well enough to ask about what was obviously a tender subject. Everyone he knew had already shut him down. He'd have to find another option.

Looking at the current time stamp, Erron cursed under his breath and rushed to clear the screen and shut down the monitor. He made a special effort to put every control and directory back the way they were. A quick check back to see Barrus still asleep did nothing to calm the guilt creeping into his chest. He should have asked to use Barrus's security access.

With an unspoken apology, Erron rushed to the door. There was just enough time to get a quick shower and to the mess hall. The day wasn't going to start itself without him.

ERRON WAS FRANTICALLY mixing the batter for the batch of waffles. For the last half hour, he'd scrambled to get the breakfast prep done, worried he wouldn't be ready for the morning meal service. Gamin had yet to arrive. Again. For a few weeks, Gamin had periodically run late, but it was becoming an expectation now. Even so, the chef had never run so late before. If Erron weren't so buried in his workload, he'd go track Gamin down.

It wasn't as if he didn't know where to find him. Last week, Erron had found Gamin in his quarters still asleep, the empty whiskey bottle on the floor and an unfinished drink on the nightstand. He hoped that this wasn't the cause for all of his tardiness, but Erron knew better. It wasn't as if he'd never seen such behavior before.

The first three weeks Erron was on board were nothing like this. It was only the past month everything spoiled. Erron had no idea what the cause was.

Erron didn't like secrets. Secrets had cost him his relationship, job, and home in one fell swoop. Secrets cost him his mother during the civil war. Secrets were being kept from him regarding who Niven Anders was and what he was to Gamin. He still saw the bright green text telling him *Access Denied* this morning.

Secrets always hurt someone in the end.

"Mrs. Claus. Give a wake-up call to—"

The kitchen door swung open and Gamin rushed inside. His clothes looked slept in and lines, probably from his sheets, had left creases on his unshaven face. Erron smelled the stale liquor. The man was marinated in it.

"Sorry I'm late." Gamin's voice was barely human. He pulled on his apron and shook his head to wake himself.

"Never mind, Mrs. Claus. For fuck's sake." Erron groused and pointed to the counter, refusing to make eye contact. "Get yourself a cup of coffee and give me a hand. I'm seriously in the weeds here."

Without another word, Gamin headed for the dispenser. "Coffee. Black. Large." The heated beverage filled the mug, and he took a huge gulp of the steaming black brew. Even with both hands, he barely held the bitter lifeline steady. With a second take, Gamin shook his head, and alertness sparked back into his eyes.

"I'll get the protein and the fruit set up. "You keep on the carbohydrates. We'll catch up fast. You've done a really good job, Erron." A sharp, sincere nod and Gamin took off on his mission, disappearing into the galley.

Erron blew a long sigh of relief as he ran his forearm across his forehead. They might actually get through this day after all.

Chapter Six

ERRON SAT IN the observation deck, located at the front of the ship in a free access area two decks below the bridge. Three tiers of theater-style chairs graced the room, which featured a series of impossibly thick hybrid plastic-glass windows, offering a one-hundred-eighty-degree view. Light panels provided a soft glow in the room, their careful placement prevented reflection on the expansive viewport surface.

Surprised at the comfort level, Erron was settled in the center seat at the top row, alive at the spectacle before him. This was the first time he'd had the chance to look out into the vastness of space and observe the universe from the inside.

The endless black made Erron feel so tiny. There was nothing like space to show a man how insignificant he was to the universe. The lack of sound coming from outside lent a surreal quality to the view. Even where there was nothing, he sensed the absence of everything. How bizarre it was to witness a true void, even with the darkness broken sporadically by the twinkle of distant galaxies. Constellations he had memorized in the night sky as a child were no longer recognizable from this vantage point. If he looked carefully, he could tell the difference between the stars and the planets within the cluster. The planets had a unique glow brighter than the rest.

The monitor on the far wall displayed the real-time flight path through the cluster. Erron studied it often, comparing the two views as the screen fluctuated between the astronomic charts and detailed information of various landmarks.

The main Subspace Link hub connecting the planets in its infinite datastream was behind the ship in relation to their destination, the planet Datham. The blue-green marble looked so tiny in the distance, but it was so much bigger than the rest of the lights in the sky. The distance was deceiving. Erron could spend days just cataloging the splendor outside the ship.

Before the *Santa Claus*, Erron had never been off-world. The idea had been a ludicrous pipe dream. Now, here he was, unsure what life planet-side possibly offered him. He had a pair of lovers—a pair, can you believe it—who treated him with respect and adoration. He'd rekindled his missing relationship with the man he'd grown up with. In spite of the growing chaos he recognized surrounding Gamin, he was in love with this ship and its crew.

"Mrs. Claus. How long before we land on Datham?"

"We should be landing at Datham Spaceport Alpha in approximately sixty-four hours, Mr. Murfin."

Erron smiled at the synthetic voice. Mrs. Claus sounded nothing like his mother, but she played a suitable surrogate. She sat in the background unseen, much like the idea of his own mother keeping watch from heaven. If the real thing wasn't available, then Mrs. Claus would do. He wondered if any of the other men saw her the same way.

A welling of melancholy came to the surface, just like it always did when Erron thought of his mother. He missed her so much, and he lost her far too early. Stacy Murfin would have spotted Toby, the smarmy bastard, a kilometer away because she had known when Erron had chosen a loser. Experience was her guide, if not her own good sense. She should have been there to tell him to stay away from Toby and save him the heartache. Mustering up a stern motherly force, she'd have chased him off long before he made a mess out of Erron's life.

Was she out there somewhere among the stars, flitting about from planet to planet looking over him as he voyaged across the cluster? Erron hoped so. Her life had been hard enough. The idea her afterlife was the same was an unbearable thought.

"I miss you, Mom. You were supposed to be around a lot longer than this. I hope you're out there listening." Erron rubbed the back of his hand along his eyes before the tears fell.

A strong pair of hands gently squeezed his shoulders from behind. "I'm sure she is. I can't imagine anyone who cared for you not wanting to watch over you." He didn't even need to look or hear the voice to know it was Barrus. Erron had come to know the unique weight of his touch in such a short time.

Without looking up, Erron covered Barrus's hand with his own and leaned into his forearm. The heat along his neck and face made the sadness a little smaller than his place in the universe.

"Am I interrupting anything? Privacy can be hard to come by on this boat."

"No."

"Are you okay?"

Erron nodded. "I will be."

Barrus's firm thumbs kneaded the stress from Erron's shoulders. The basic, rhythmic pressure softened him like warm butter into the chair. It reminded Erron no matter how much he longed to hear his mother's voice again, there were loving people in his life to make up for the loss.

Erron purred with this kind of attention. "I'll give you exactly three hours to stop that, sir." A pleasant shiver rushed down his spine, making his eyes roll back into his head.

A soft, lusty chuckle graced Erron's ear. "I aim to please." Barrus completed his massage, his roaming hands coming to rest on Erron's chest. The gentle kiss he placed atop the crown of Erron's head, a caring signature.

"Since this is your first port of call, have you decided how you want to spend your time in Datham?"

"I promised Gamin we'd tour the spaceport. Get dinner, see a vid, do the special purchasing. Basically make a day of it."

Barrus's hands went still. "You're spending the whole time with Gamin?"

Erron twisted to look up at Barrus's face. A stoic expression sat there, the perfect poker face in contrast to the tension he felt. Bit by bit, Barrus's eyes gave him away with a hint of...disappointment?

Climbing onto his knees in the chair, Erron placed a hand along Barrus's stubbled jaw. "Since I was a little kid, Gamin always promised to someday take me traveling to another world. When he left after he and Mom had their falling out, I never thought I'd get that chance. I didn't see him for over twelve years. Now he's here again, and he has the chance to make good on his promise."

Barrus's shoulders and expression sagged. "It's just that James and I wanted to take you out for a real date for a change."

"There will be other ports that we can take advantage of. Since the three of us grouped up, I haven't spent much time with him. Gamin and I lost touch for a long time and something's not quite right. He's not happy and I think he needs this."

Barrus's gaze drifted away and he was unusually quiet. Erron felt his discontent. Reaching his arms around the big man's neck, he leaned forward until their foreheads came into light contact.

"Hey." Erron tried to track Barrus's gaze back to his own. "Please don't be upset. I should have told you sooner. I have a bit of a blind spot where Gamin's concerned. He's all I have left of my family."

"We want to be your family too." Barrus's voice was barely a whisper, but the frustration screamed out loud.

Erron turned Barrus's face, peering deep into his brown eyes. "And if I thought sharing with Gamin right now was a good idea, I'd make it a group deal. There's a lot going on around him that really worries me."

"What's going on?"

"I don't want to say until I can stir up the nerve to talk to Gamin first. I owe him that much. You just have to trust me on this."

Barrus sighed. "James is going to be really unhappy. He had a private spa he wanted to take you to."

"I'll make it up to you both. I promise. You let James know at the next port, I will do whatever he asks for." A playful grin curled Erron's mouth. "Even that perverted thing he keeps asking for from me."

"You may regret offering that up. For some things, James is kind of a like a dog with a favorite bone."

"Now that's an appropriate description. If it helps Gamin, it will be worth it. He's that important to me." Erron raised his right hand as if swearing an oath. "I promise I'll keep my chastity belt on at all times, sir."

The deep resonating laugh that burst out of Barrus disarmed Erron's nerves. He wanted to kick himself for not thinking of his partners when he made the plans for shore leave. It was selfish and shortsighted, but Barrus appeared to have forgiven him. Although, he foresaw a lot of begging and pleading in his future. He didn't need the phony seer from the space station diner to tell him that. In the end, everything would be fine.

"Don't give me any ideas, you little imp. Who knew dating you meant dating Gamin too." Surrounding him with his brawny arms, Barrus gave him a firm hug. A jealous undertone tinted his words, so Erron made a silent promise to try not to stoke it any further. All of the men in his life were important to him.

"He comes with the package, Barrus. I've known him my entire life. You guys have to accept that or move on."

Barrus brushed a soft kiss on Erron's lips. "We're not going anywhere, Erron. Accept that."

THE MARKET DISTRICT in Datham's spaceport was so much different from the one on Alpha Centauri. While endless lines of shops and boutiques displayed their wares, an equal number of artisan vendors were found amongst the higher-end proprietors as well. Even though Erron had never been off world before, he was familiar with the cluster's history. After the Great Migration from Earth so many centuries ago, Datham had been primarily founded by manufacturing companies and artisans. The architecture and design were stylish and well crafted but lacked the excessive opulence one expected from other planets, such as Luxoria. Everywhere Erron looked, there was a graceful beauty quietly beckoning to him.

The morning had been spent with Gamin, touring the station and acquiring special food items for the *Santa Claus*. Erron knew James had always arranged a standing budget for the chef to buy unique ingredients to keep life interesting on board. Even in his short time on board, he knew no one ever complained about a repetitious menu. Gamin had also noted the budget had increased on this trip, grumbling under his breath it was probably due to Erron sleeping with the supply officer.

Once the ship's purchases were complete, Gamin escorted the loaded pallet back to the ship while Erron continued to shop. It had been awhile since he'd had any currency worth noting in his accounts and now was the time to take advantage of the locale. With the port teeming with possible shops, he could hardly resist. Gamin made plans with him to meet for a late lunch after he'd taken care of the perishable groceries.

There were so many boutiques to choose from. The first two Erron set foot in were far outside his budget or the clothing was too elaborate to be practical for a cook on a transport cruiser. The snobbish attitudes of the shopkeepers also helped Erron make his mind up to spend his money elsewhere.

Following a man dressed in laborer's clothing, Erron found a perfect garment shop. The clothing looked colorful—but not garish—with an earthy quality, well crafted and sensible. Catering to men exclusively, the store seemed endless in its choices. He knew he'd be there for a while. With a quick com to Gamin to let him know where he was, Erron set off on his new adventure.

It felt good to collect some new clothing. Erron was a little embarrassed to admit how little he had to work with when he came on board. A large portion of his wardrobe had been purchased by Toby, and every one of those items found their way into the incinerator when he'd been evicted. If the dress code on the *Santa Claus* wasn't so relaxed, he'd have been mortified. Even so, Erron was not about to stay the ragtag street urchin forever.

The shop's pricing was good, so Erron assembled a quick collection of basic gear. New shirts and breeches, as well as shorts and shoes, made the cut. Looking at the pile, Erron felt a little bit better about himself.

Erron acknowledged his guilt over spoiling James's plans for this stop, but he really needed to spend some time with Gamin. When he first came on board, Gamin had monopolized his time, and now James and Barrus were doing the same. Erron missed watching vids and catching up with the chef outside of the kitchen. He would have to do something to balance out the discrepancy.

Thinking of James reminded him he needed some new undergarments. After he had made a few comments about how all of Erron's briefs looked alike, he decided he'd better get some more to hide the fact he owned so few. Going without wasn't a good choice for him.

On one display, he found the type he liked. The style was simple, basic, and well made. Distinctly masculine in dark earthy tones but definitely sexy. The synthetic fabric was soft and pliable, and Erron loved the way it wrapped itself around his fingers as he handled the sample. It was bound to hug his figure, and there was ample give in the front to comfortably hold and display his package. Finding underwear that didn't bind had always been a challenge.

"That's a little more brazen than what I'm used to seeing you in," Gamin chided.

Gamin's teasing lit a fire so bright in Erron his cheeks could have signaled a dozen cruisers across the cluster. He stood like a fool, handling the undergarment while Gamin smirked with an impish gleam in his eye. For some reason, the memory of the chastity oath he joked to Barrus flashed through his mind. It took a serious effort not to burst into a fit of schoolgirl laughter.

"I have to choose something." Erron placed the sample garment back on the display. "Otherwise, James is likely to outfit me in some kind of fetish gear I'm just not prepared for."

Gamin's mischievous smile dissolved into a polite but flat facade. "Well, we don't want that to happen."

Erron picked out a few more pairs, adding them to the pile, while he swore Gamin made an effort not to watch. It had to be horrifically comical to watch him carry the disheveled pile of clothing to the cashier.

"Not doing it small, are you?" Gamin eyed the tower of garments with a raised brow as Erron attempted to keep it from tipping over.

"Not a whole lot of a choice, really. Toby liked me to dress a certain way, so I burned everything he ever bought me when he cut me loose. It didn't leave me with much afterward. At the time, I was too pissed off to think it through."

Gamin shrugged in assent. "I get that. Come on. Let's get you processed so we can get something to eat. There's actually a few decent places to eat here that don't rape your account."

Thankfully, the cashier made quick work of the transaction, finalizing the payment with a DNA ID scan. Next, they loaded everything onto an automated valet cart that whisked Erron's purchases back to the *Santa Claus* as part of the shop's service. Gamin led the way, checking the station map on his handheld com pad, as they wound through the maze of vendors and lifts.

"Are we lost?" Erron was sure they were walking in a circle.

"No."

"So where are we going? I'm getting hungry."

"It's a special place. I haven't been here in a long time."

The answer was vague, but Erron trusted Gamin, so he followed without protest. He didn't have an appetite for breakfast after the *Santa Claus* landed, and now his stomach was making noises. Finally, in a less-populated area off the main district, they found themselves in front of the Sprits Grille.

Erron liked what he saw.

Every square centimeter exuded an aura of comfort and beauty. Ceramic tiles in shades of green, rust, and gold lined the walls, each slightly irregular with minor flaws. Tabletops made of stone slabs with forged metal bases were softened with warm tapestry runners flowing over the sides, yet exposing the construction on the edges. The restaurant was half-full of patrons eating and chatting in the gentle atmospheric light. How could you get that luminescence from an artificial source? Everything about the cafe screamed craftsmanship and artistry. It was an amazing secret nestled amongst the bazaar trade existing not so far away.

At Gamin's request, the host, a thin yet rugged man of no more than twenty years, sat them at a booth away from the main throng of customers. As he settled in, Erron's chair seemed to mold to his body while the hint of jasmine and savory meals stroked his senses. Gamin's eyes came alive in the ambient light as he shared his treasure. The glow set off his features, proving the gray in Gamin's hair failed to diminish how handsome he was.

Erron's breath was taken away. "This is beautiful."

"It certainly is." Gamin's vision was fixed on his dining partner. A fresh heat appeared in Erron's cheeks. A smile curled his lips as he cleared his throat and shifted away from direct eye contact. Surreptitiously, he let out a breath to calm his quickening heartbeat.

"Afternoon, gentlemen. I'm Leif. I'll be taking care of you today. Can I start you off with anything to drink?"

"I'll have a whiskey. Make it a double."

Erron's brow flattened. "Just Brusha tea."

Leif paused, glancing at Erron for the briefest moment before nodding and heading to fulfill their order.

Gamin's brow cocked with a touch of confusion. "Is something wrong? You seem annoyed somehow."

"Whiskey? With lunch?"

Gamin shrugged. "It's my day off. I'm relaxing. You're welcome to relax a little too."

"I don't drink."

"Really? How did that not come up on the ship?"

"It just didn't." Erron's tone was harsher than he intended, but he refused to apologize for it.

"Look, Erron. I don't want to make an issue of this. I want to spend a little time with you. It's still like we have so much catching up to do. We don't get too many opportunities like this with our job."

As much as Erron didn't want to admit it, Gamin was right. Days off would be a rarity for them as long as he was part of the crew, and he didn't see it changing anytime soon. That discussion could wait until later. He resolved himself to enjoying the meal and the company.

"You're right. What should we have?" Touching a small panel mounted to the table, a holographic menu appeared. The selection was simple, but the choices were promising. If Gamin liked this place, the food had to be worth it.

Gamin reached over and turned off Erron's menu as he activated his own. "My treat, my surprise." With a few quick touches while paging through the menu, Gamin ordered for them both. They didn't have to wait long for the young man who sat them to reappear.

Leif served the drinks, pinning a wary glance at Erron. He politely excused himself, vowing to return when the food was ready.

Gamin took a strong sip of his whiskey. "I double-checked this place is still owned by the same family, and the same chef is responsible for the food. Every morsel is hand-prepared. You can taste it. You'll love this place." The more Gamin spoke about the restaurant, the more animated he became.

"All right. I'll take your word for it." Any doubt Erron had vanished as he took a sip of his tea. It was lovely how complex the flavors were. Licking his lips to savor it, he found Gamin focused on his every moment.

"The food is even better."

Gamin was right. Every bite of every course was nirvana. Even simple dishes were culinary works of art they carefully sampled and devoured. Keeping quiet under the succulent pleasures was a task in itself. Looking absolutely smug, Gamin sat across the table sporting a wolfish grin. With another round of drinks and a dessert order into the kitchen, Gamin's mood turned serious.

"I don't want to sour the meal, but I've been meaning to ask you about your mother. There's never been a good time to ask. Even after all these years, I still miss her."

"It's okay. I've been thinking a lot about her lately. I wish I knew more about what happened between you two."

Gamin's gaze dropped to the table as his brow creased harshly. "That's not a story I want to tell. Someday. Just not today. Please?"

Erron nodded.

Gamin took a hard swallow of his whiskey before asking, "Do you mind if I ask what happened to her?"

"It's pretty simple." Erron sighed as he voiced the words he'd repeated in his mind far too many times over the years. "She drank too much. Sudden liver failure after years of systematic alcohol abuse. Or so the autopsy scan notes said." Looking away, Erron sipped the last of his tea. Some memories were hard to face.

Gamin's mouth gaped in shock. "How did that happen?"

"You really need to ask?"

"You said she died in a raid."

"It's a lot easier to say out loud than 'My mom was an addict.'"

"I knew Stacy liked to have a good time, but I'd never have guessed…"

Erron shrugged and pushed his hair behind his ear. "It's not that hard to imagine. When it's someone that close, I think you tend to blind yourself to how self-destructive they can be. She functioned well, held down a job, paid the bills, and did it all with a drink in hand. I think we told ourselves she was fine because it was easier than the alternative. How do you confront your mother like that?"

A swell of unhappy memories came to the surface. No man should have to remember the nights of cleaning up his mother after she fell asleep in her own sick. Or the incoherent conversations swilled in cheap liquor, laced with volatile swings of anger and sobbing. Or hiding the evidence from friends and neighbors because the shame was so great. It was no wonder alcohol held no allure for Erron.

"Stacy had to have known how sick she was getting."

"Maybe. But once we were in the middle of the civil war, I wasn't there to keep an eye on her. I got drafted into the Army Corps when it broke out. I wrote her and told her I was on cooking detail and wasn't seeing any action. I think it still scared her and that it just made matters worse. I was in the middle of a meal service when I got the death notice."

"A doctor could have fixed her up easy."

Taking a deep breath, Erron caught Gamin's eyes and poured his stare into them. "You have to go to the doctor and actually listen to what they have to say for them to help. Then she'd have had to admit there was a problem. Her skills at denial were legendary. Mom was nothing if not stubborn."

A long quiet descended. Even when the waiter brought the mouth-watering dessert to the table, neither man uttered a word. Poor Leif was positively awkward as he stepped away. Erron felt awful at the host-waiter's discomfort, but the conversation's turn had left him conflicted. Why did his conversations with Gamin always have the prospect of scalding them? Why was it so hard?

Gamin broke the silence. "Speaking of doctors, are you still seeing Dr. Bosch regularly?"

"Yeah. He has me scheduled to stop in every other week now." Erron's response was ragged, but he didn't mind the subject shift. In fact, he welcomed it.

The tenor of the conversation had changed, but Erron was ashamed that the trip had taken such a turn. This was supposed to be a day of fun, and now it was tainted with unspoken issues. While he was happy that the direction had changed to better topics, he regretted his inability to voice his concerns. Whatever Erron had expected or planned from this excursion, he lost the will to be direct. Now that the opportunity had passed, he'd have to find another avenue to ask the important questions. *Coward.*

"You get used to it. Bosch is overly thorough. Once he has you settled in, it'll kick back to every other month."

Erron sighed. "I have an appointment with him tomorrow night after we leave Datham. He wants to double-check how I'm handling the takeoff, along with everything else."

"Well, listen to what he says. He's a good man and takes good care of us."

HIDDEN BEHIND THE privacy screens, Erron sat undressed on the sick-bay bed, trying to pretend being examined was natural. He focused on the chimes of the scanners and the hum of the ship engines to drown out how he felt like a laboratory animal after every appointment. As a new recruit, the company policy stated he was subject to regular exams until completely cleared. Erron ignored the jokes amongst the crew about how the doctor always got the "new boys" first. Given Dr. Bosch's professional manner, Erron was pretty sure he ignored them too.

Dr. Bosch tapped a code into the small cylindrical device before touching it to Erron's bare shoulder. When he pressed the trigger, Erron gave an odd shiver as the transdermal surge of meds fed into his system. Erron checked, like he did every time, to see if a mark had been left behind.

"That finishes up your inoculations and antivirals. You're now covered for all known diseases and infections, including sexually transmitted."

Erron's brow rose dramatically. "Sexual infections? Really, Doc?"

"You have met this crew, haven't you?"

"Hmm... Good point."

"You can go ahead and get dressed, Erron."

The slender blond doctor walked over to one of the monitors to read the scan output. Erron thought it was odd he wasn't leaving the room while he dressed, but when it was obvious the doctor wasn't paying attention to him, he shrugged it off and began pulling on his clothes.

"Can I ask you a weird question?"

The doctor responded without turning around. "Of course."

Erron ground his teeth slightly as he struck up the nerve to ask. "Can anyone's DNA scan open anyone else's quarters?"

"Other than a security bypass, no. Do you think someone's been in your quarters?"

"No. Nothing like that. I was just wondering if there was any other way someone could get in other than a bypass."

"The only other way I can think of is if a blood relative keyed open the door. DNA ID might be close enough to fool the sensor, but we don't have any of those on board."

Erron froze for a moment as he buckled his breeches. He chewed his lip for a minute, shook the ridiculous notion brewing out of his head, and continued. He was just pulling on one of his newly purchased shirts when the doctor finally turned to face him.

"How have you been feeling? You're showing an elevated blood pressure level, higher than when you first arrived on board."

"Really? I'm fine."

Bosch's eyes narrowed slightly. "How about dizzy spells? Are you having any of those?"

"No. I'm fine."

"Are you under a lot of stress lately?"

Erron gave off a heavy sigh. "I guess so. I mean, the workload is heavier than I expected, but I really enjoy it. James and Barrus have been great, but they're starting to show a bit of jealousy over my friendship with Gamin. And he's been doing the same with them. There's not enough of me to go around. And...well...Gamin's drinking has really got me worried."

"How so?"

"This is confidential, right?"

The doctor nodded.

"Gamin keeps coming in late for shifts smelling like a distillery and I keep seeing him with a drink more and more often. I've found him rip drunk on more than one occasion. It seems like it's getting worse. Is there anything you can do for him, Doc?"

"Are you sure you're seeing what you think you're seeing?"

Erron snarled in annoyance. "I know what addiction looks like, Doctor. I grew up with it."

The doctor raised a hand in apology. "I can't really discuss the medical details of any of the crew, including you, without permission. If there is a substance problem—and I'm not saying there is—I can take care of the physical damage long-term abuse can cause. But if the patient isn't ready to confront their problem, it won't make a bit of difference because they'll undo the work I've done. I can't cure the psychological triggers that can cause the abuse. That's their job."

"I think it has something to do with Niven."

A small crease formed between the doctor's brows and his tone became focused. "Niven Anders? What has Gamin told you about Niven?"

Erron grumbled. "Same as everyone else. Nothing."

"Then you can imagine how asking his doctor about that would be even less likely to work. Confidentiality, remember?"

Erron threw his hands up in frustration as his voice rose. "I won't say I'm surprised. I can't get anyone to fucking tell me anything and his file has a security lock." Exhaling sharply, he scrubbed a hand through his hair as his shoulders deflated. "I need to know what's going on. My mother drank herself to death. I'm really scared I might lose him too."

The doctor closed the gap between them and placed a comforting hand on Erron's shoulder. In true professional bedside fashion, he offered a hopeful voice.

"Then perhaps you should make your case to the Head of Security."

ERRON LOST TRACK of how many minutes he stood in front of Room 204, unsure of what to do. The dull metal of the door seemed to mock his indecision with its lackluster finish in the way it hid its occupants inside. A pounding noise invaded his ears. It was his heartbeat. Added to the clammy chill on his brow, Erron was mere moments from having an anxiety attack.

So much had gone awry when he asked Gamin about Niven before. Was this going to be just another thing that backfired?

Please let that not be the case.

"Mrs. Claus. Where can I find Sergeant Liam Jacks?"

"Sergeant Jacks can be found in his quarters. Room 204," she repeated for the third time.

Erron rubbed his thumbs along his clenched fingers as he continued to stare at the door's control panel. The prospect of possibly finding his answers was driving him crazy. If he found himself staring at another firewall, it would kill him. He needed to know what role Niven played in Gamin's life. Once he understood, he might be able to help. This was for Gamin.

With a deep breath, he reluctantly reached for the black plexiglass panel mounted to the hull, ignoring the tremor in his hand.

The door slid open, leaving Erron standing there like a fool, his hand just short of the control. He found himself staring into a bare, chiseled chest composed of smooth olive skin. The man in the door was physically flawless, his only visible hair being his eyebrows and a manicured goatee. A sheer blue sarong, tied low at the waist, clung indecently to the generous organ between his legs. The only other adornment was a metal armband on his left arm, landing below the shoulder, an elaborate tattoo oddly disappearing beneath it. Trying not to gawk, Erron raised his chin, finding himself staring into the prettiest ice-blue eyes he'd ever seen.

"You are Erron Murfin, the new crewman." The man's voice was velvet smooth with a hint of foreign accent. It made Erron want to melt.

Erron shook himself into the present. "Y...Yes. You're Hadrian Jamison, right? I still haven't gotten to know the whole crew. I heard you were ill when I first came on board."

"I am fine, Erron." Hadrian glanced at the metal band around his arm. "Is there something I can help you with?"

The words started and stalled on his lips three times before he forced them out in a rush. "I was wondering if I could speak with Sergeant Jacks."

A soft smile graced Hadrian's lips. "Of course. Come in, Erron."

Hadrian turned and stepped into the room. Erron fought not to fixate on the distracting sway of hard flesh on display before him. Every movement was somehow arousing as if the man was taught how to be alluring without trying.

The quarters had been turned into a sitting room. It had somewhat haphazard furnishings but was strangely comfortable. An open doorway had been added along one wall, connecting the adjacent quarters, creating a master suite. Hadrian motioned Erron to sit in an armchair as he stepped into the bedroom.

"There is someone here to see you, Liam."

In the mirror's reflection along the wall, an enormous man took a pair of listening devices out of his ears, stood up, and pulled a pair of shorts over a muscular lower half in a black jockstrap. He came around and through the doorway, and Erron felt insignificant before the hulking security chief.

"Mr. Murfin." Liam spoke with a polite smile. "What can I help you with?"

Erron had served all of the crew at one time or another since becoming a member, but this was different. The tight T-shirt stretched over Liam's enormous torso and the glimpse he had just caught of Liam's impressive backside was sidetracking his purpose. The man was big, powerful, and intimidating and had a partner men would fight over for the chance to spend five minutes with. He'd never been this close to the couple before. The serving line always provided a buffer between them. Keeping on task shouldn't have been this hard.

Erron spun his gaze to the floor. "Gamin. I need to talk to you about Gamin."

"Is something wrong?" Liam sat in the chair opposite Erron while Hadrian took position behind his partner.

"I'm really worried about him." Thoughts of Gamin sobered Erron at once. "He's been drinking so heavily. I'm worried about his health."

"Have you spoken with Gamin about this?"

"It's not that simple. Gamin's really important to me. He's family. I need to understand what's happening better before I can confront him."

Liam shook his head slightly. "I don't see how I'm

supposed to help. If the ship or crew isn't at risk, there isn't a lot I can do."

"Whatever is going on, I think Niven Anders is the reason."

Erron noticed how taut the sergeant's physique became. Niven's name had struck a jagged chord. Even Hadrian's head tilted in Liam's direction as if he heard something unspoken.

"Niven?" Liam's face grew tight. "What did Gamin tell you about him?"

"The same as everyone else on this ship: absolutely fucking nothing. I mentioned him once and Gamin got so sad and upset he didn't speak to me for almost two days. I know there's something about Niven that hurts Gamin badly. I need to know what, if I'm going to help him."

"What do you need me for?"

"There's a security lock on Niven's personnel file. Even his information on the Link is redirected back to a firewall. No one will tell me anything about him. Nothing. I'm asking you to unlock it so I can piece together what's going on."

The longer the conversation went on, the more agitated Liam appeared. "I don't see how that will help."

"Gamin's drinking is getting worse. I see it every day. I need to know what happened with Niven that he can't let go."

Liam crossed his large arms over his chest. The defensive posture screamed refusal. "Gamin is a grown man. We look out for him and he takes care of us. He'll be fine."

"*No, he won't!*" Erron jumped to his feet, nearly overturning the chair. "I don't know why everyone's trying to hide what happened, but all you're doing is enabling Gamin." Erron's voice cracked as his eyes welled. "I know this is a huge invasion of privacy and I probably don't have any right to ask. But I already lost my mother to addiction. I can't lose Gamin too."

Hadrian reached up and squeezed Liam's shoulder. "If it helps Gamin, will it be harmful to tell Erron, Liam? I can sense how upsetting this topic is. Is this a secret worth keeping?"

Liam furrowed his brow as he crushed his eyes closed. He slumped into the chair and slowly edged his head back and forth in indecision. With an audible exhale, Liam opened his eyes, unable to disguise the pain radiating from them. Growling in frustration, he pawed at his face and through his tight crop of auburn hair with both hands.

"I don't need to open the file." Liam motioned Erron to sit back down. "I can tell you everything that's in it. I wrote it."

"I'm sorry. I don't mean to cause more trouble."

"It's not your fault. I've never been very fond of dredging up my memories."

Chapter Seven

FOUR YEARS, FIVE MONTHS AGO

"How do you like the *Santa Claus* so far, Niven?"

"Way better than being in the Marines, Sergeant Jacks." Broad, energetic, and standing at Liam's shoulder, Niven's shaved head sported a small spike of dark hair at the top, matching the spike of growth off his chin. Bright, youthful blue eyes somehow gleamed in the artificial light of the *Santa Claus*'s hallway. Liam tried not to find himself distracted by Niven's infectious jovial mood or the tight body stretching the gray sleeveless shirt.

"I told you, call me Liam."

Niven's shrug was animated. "Sorry. Some habits don't die easy."

Niven Anders was the newest crew member on board. Most of the morning had been spent in close quarters with Liam as he acquainted Niven with the ship's layout and the various security protocols he was responsible for. The task had taken hours, and while Liam found the procedure mind-numbing at times, Niven was alive and excited by every aspect.

"That's okay. It'll happen soon enough. A lot of us on board are ex-military. Captain Danverse bought the ship after the civil war ended and the government bought out our contracts. It was a better option than staying on planet. Some of us couldn't stomach the military after the war."

Liam paused, remembering his own history of the Alpha Centauri Civil War. "I read your record. You stayed on afterward."

"I was in demolitions. It took a long time to find all that hidden ordinance and defuse it. Didn't really seem right to go until the job was done. Besides, the job security and pay were good."

"Well, I'm glad you got out. The career span in that department wasn't exactly long term."

Niven's eyes darkened slightly. "Yeah. I lost a few friends over it, but I sleep better knowing I removed so many explosives. I took one out from a schoolyard once, can you believe it? Makes me sick sometimes just thinking about it."

"I can understand." Liam's own wartime memories flashed to the front and the guilt tried to drown him. The child casualties never sat well.

"Enough of that depressing shit." Niven thumped Liam's shoulder with his strong fist. The somber conversational tone vanished and became something far more upbeat. "It's my first day on the *Santa Claus* and I'm having a good day."

Broken from his reverie, Liam shook himself and broke out with a grin. "You're right. Let's get some food. It's the first meal service after takeoff and Gamin usually treats us special."

"Now that's what I'm talking about." Niven licked his lips and wrung his hands together.

After exiting the lift, Liam's stomach screamed its hunger aloud when the most savory scent filled the hall, tempting his palate. Gamin was far too gifted a chef to be wasted on this crew, but Liam was damned if he was about to steer the man away.

Niven's mouth fell open as soon as he caught the aroma. "Holy shit, I'm salivating already."

"And you haven't even tasted it yet."

"Then let's not be rude and take too long to get there." Like an overgrown child, Niven sprinted down the hall with Liam laughing behind him. He didn't need to tell the newbie where they were going. The smell would have pointed the way if they'd been blindfolded. He only stopped just short of the mess hall's entrance to allow Liam to catch up.

The cafeteria was well populated tonight, and Niven turned quite a few heads as he entered. Several sets of appreciative eyes scanned him top to bottom. The men did love the sight of a new boy in town.

Liam leaned in and whispered, "Beware. The wolves are circling."

Niven turned his back on his onlookers, his charming smile honest and warm. "They can circle all they like. I'm very particular about who I take to bed. Let's hope they're not too disappointed."

Liam led his protégé to the buffet line while a number of men introduced themselves to Niven on the way. This was nothing new to Liam. In fact, he was expecting it. With how tight-knit their little community could be, there was no surprise at how much the crew enjoyed the sport of a new arrival. It was impressive how polite and personable Niven was as he wove his way through the crowd without actually giving any of the men tangible hope for a rendezvous. Niven was a pretty smooth character.

Once they finally made it to the serving line, they grabbed trays and made a path to Gamin, who was personally serving this evening. Apron bearing stains from the night's offerings, the large chef was in good spirits. He joked and laughed with each man in line, and seemed to be having the time of his life.

"What can I offer you tonight, Sergeant?"

"Why don't you pick, Gamin? I'm in the mood to be surprised." Gamin filled a plate with several dishes, each one looking better than the last. So entranced by the future meal, it took a moment to register why Gamin continued to glance back and forth between himself and Niven.

"Oh! Shit!" Liam shook his head. "I'm sorry, Gamin. I'd like you to meet Niven Anders. He's our new addition to security."

A Cheshire grin stretched across Gamin's face as he reached across the line and shook hands with the new arrival. "It's nice to meet you, Niven."

"The pleasure's mine, Big Daddy." Niven's grin was so intense it risked burning itself into place. Even his cheeks were starting to flush.

Liam turned to Niven with an arched eyebrow. "Big Daddy?"

"What would you like?" Gamin's gaze was locked on Niven.

"Chef's choice. Everything looks good from here." Niven wasn't even looking at the food options. The scene was a touch awkward, so Liam cleared his throat. Gamin and Niven both chuckled as they broke eye contact. With a lively bounce, Gamin served up a plate and added an extra serving before passing it over.

"Here you go, boy. I gave you a little extra. A man like you needs to keep up your strength around here." Gamin's indecent smile was scorching as he turned to the next person in line, leaving Niven standing still just staring.

Liam rolled his eyes and put a finger in the man's belt loop, tugging him sideways.

"Come on, Niven. It's time to eat." Laughing, he led the young man away from the serving line while the new crewman shot looks over his shoulder at Gamin. They found an open table together and tucked in. Niven had yet to stop smiling.

FOUR YEARS, FOUR MONTHS AGO

Somewhere around 01:30 hours, Liam had been ripped from his sleep. Another devastating nightmare had left him sweaty and quaking in the dark. He knew he wouldn't sleep afterward. The things he'd seen and done during the Alpha Centauri Civil War still haunted him. If only he knew a way to smother the guilt.

He was still shaking when he entered the gymnasium and pounded the boxing dummy and the treadmill relentlessly until he was a heaving mess. Perspiration soaked his clothes and skin. His body sat at the edge of exhaustion, but the dream's effects had yet to calm down. Liam slumped down into a wayward corner and pressed the buds of his tech into his ears, turning up the music to drown out the shame.

It was sometime after 04:00 hours when he finally lowered the volume. Some semblance of his sanity had been restored and he needed to start being human again. Sleep was gone, but he could start his rounds early and get back into his routine. It was a small gift no one had entered and found him huddled in the corner at this late hour. He had no idea how to explain it.

His body protested as he pried himself from the floor. With muscles like lead, he ambled across the room. Liam would ache tomorrow, but he didn't care. It was the least he deserved for the things he'd done during the war.

The sweat had dried on his skin long ago, making the grime in every pore more obvious. If there was any hope of salvaging the day, he needed to be clean. The locker room was empty, so Liam stripped off. It was difficult to remove his sticky pair of shorts and T-shirt. Rolling his clammy jockstrap down his thick legs, he grabbed a towel from the linen-storage bin. With the music still playing through his earpieces, Liam didn't notice someone else was already in the shower.

It wasn't what he was expecting. Liam might not have been able to hear, but he read the words on his lips perfectly.

"Fuck me, Big Daddy."

In stunned silence, Liam unconsciously reached up and touched off the tech in his ears. Niven's chest was pressed against the shower wall, the spray raining down over him, while Gamin knelt, feasting in the cleft of Niven's backside. Eyes closed, throaty, mewling spilled out of Niven as he tried to grip the smooth wall. Gamin's strong hands squeezed and pried the meaty globes apart, ignoring Niven's plea, seemingly determined to chew and lick deeper than anyone ever had before.

Niven's words devolved into begging. "Please, Big Daddy."

At once, Gamin pulled back and stood. He pressed his thick cock between Niven's haunches and held him still as the younger man tried to arch back into him. The blunt head was kissing the opening, but he refused to push forward.

"Is this what you want, boy?" Gamin spoke as he bit and chewed at Niven's shoulders. His burly chest and hands held Niven in place while he kept his hips away at a teasing distance.

A shudder ran through the smaller man. "Please. I need you."

Gamin spit into his hand and wet his shaft. "Take it, boy." Shifting his weight forward, he sank into the pleading man. An ecstasy-laden howl sang from Niven's mouth, growing in intensity with the depth of Gamin's invasion. It took no time before he was ready, and Gamin gave him what he asked for in a firm, pounding cadence.

Liam knew he shouldn't be watching, but he was hypnotized. The rumor was Niven wasn't with, and hadn't been with, anyone since his arrival last month. Liam had been impressed with the young man's resolve not to succumb to the men's advances. It was clear this was not a chance encounter. In spite of the heat emanating from them, their shared touches were filled with familiarity. How they'd managed to keep this a secret was beyond him.

As arousing as the raunchy action in front of him was, Liam longed for the kind of connection that bred intimacy. The only person these days he had any regular contact with was his best friend, the captain. However, that contact was nothing like this. A liaison between Liam and the captain was punishment and absolution, not passion and more.

Gamin pulled back and spun Niven around. Their lips met as they snaked their arms around each other. Niven wrapped his legs around Gamin's waist as he was lowered to the shower-room floor. A muffled moan of need passed between them as Gamin found his aim and re-entered.

Water continued to wet down the writhing men as their tempo increased. The sound of bodies slapping together, in sync with soft noises, echoed off the walls. Holding himself upright on his arms, Gamin gave Niven a punishing fuck. Each thrust was met with Niven's grunting approval. With a brutal grip on Gamin's arms, he arched into the piston beat.

Niven cried out. "Oh God. Don't stop. Whatever you do, don't stop!"

Somehow, Gamin picked up even more speed and power as a long, escalating wail escaped from Niven. Every muscle stood out in stark relief as Niven came, firing a series of pearlescent volleys between them. Gamin crushed his mouth over Niven's as he took his turn and unloaded with a muffled wail.

Gamin's whisper was audible with the room's acoustics. "Are you all right? I didn't hurt you, did I?"

Niven gently shook his head as he laid soft kisses to Gamin's face. "I'm perfect."

As they slowly came down from their high, Gamin finally noticed the other man among them.

"Oh...hello, Sergeant. Sorry, we don't share."

Niven finally caught sight of Liam. His face flushed beyond the sex, and he buried his face in Gamin's chest, completely mortified. "Um...hey, Liam."

The haze of guilt, envy, and horniness muddled his thoughts. "I'm sorry. I shouldn't have been watching. It's been a rough night, and you caught me by surprise."

The men disengaged and took position under the running showerhead. Rather than take separate spots, they shared the same one, Gamin stroking the crown of Niven's head as the water washed over him.

"No. It's our fault. We didn't plan this. It just sort of happened."

Liam snorted. "You mean sex in a public room on the ship? Or you two getting together? You're not trying to convince me this was your first time together, are you?"

Niven shook his head. "It's such a small town here, Liam. We just wanted to get to know each other without the rumors and talk."

"I can understand that."

"Can we keep this just between us? We've been getting together early before Gamin's shift so we can avoid most of the crew. We're not ready to be completely public yet."

Liam took residence at a showerhead far enough away to give the pair as much privacy as one could get in the large open room. His swollen erection wasn't the easiest thing to hide, but Gamin and Niven both had noticed it and went about their business, saying nothing. Liam turned his body away to try to show a small amount of respect in spite of his uncharacteristic voyeurism.

"I won't say a word to anyone if you don't want me to."

Gamin's smile was appreciative. "Thank you, Sergeant. We appreciate it. It won't be forever."

THREE YEARS, THREE MONTHS AGO

Captain Danverse sat at his desk in the Day Cabin with Liam and Niven seated opposite on the couch. Sipping from a glass of whiskey, he leaned back in his comfortable chair, waiting patiently for Niven to speak. Liam found himself drinking the harsh liquor in quick mouthfuls to fill the awkward silence. Niven's drink sat untouched in his hand, his thumb moving with an anxious twitch against the surface. He stared at his tapping feet with a fine sheen on his forehead. Liam had no idea why Niven had asked to speak with them, but now with the moment upon them, Niven had frozen. At this rate, Liam would be stone drunk before this meeting started, so Liam nudged him along with his free hand.

Niven jarred to life and spoke. "U...um, Captain. You know Gamin and I have been seeing each other for a while now."

"Yes, it became public knowledge after the rather infamous scene in the recreation room."

Liam added his observation. "Then there was the time they were found having sex in engineering."

"And the time you were found on your knees in the kitchen—"

"All right!" Niven dropped his head. His face and neck flushed scarlet, and he focused on a vacant spot on the floor.

Danverse held a straight face, but his eyes gleamed with mischief. "Don't worry. I've confiscated all copies of the holo made of that evening."

"I appreciate that, sir."

"You have to understand. A group of men this size with no parental figure to nag them constantly are prone to occasional fits of adolescent behavior. You just can't give them this kind of ammunition if you want to keep your relationship's activities quiet."

"I understand, sir. But that's not what I wanted to talk to you about."

Danverse grinned. "Oh. Then by all means. Go right ahead."

Steeling himself, Niven took a deep breath and an even deeper drink. Liam knew the captain was toying with Niven, but he was far too amused to say anything. Yet.

Niven started and stopped, then blurted everything out. "I want to marry Gamin. I want us to live here on the *Santa Claus*. While we were in port last week, I bought him a ring."

Pleased, yet confused, Liam broke in. "If you're planning on living on the ship, why am I here?"

Niven gave Liam a sheepish grin. "Moral support. You introduced us."

"Have you asked him yet?" Danverse's smirk had yet to fade.

Niven shook his head. "Not yet."

"Why not?"

"First, I need to know if you'll marry us, Captain. It wouldn't be right not to have the ceremony here on board."

Danverse set down his drink and steepled his hands as his tone sobered. "You realize, of course, that a ship captain's privilege to marry a couple is strictly an old-world tradition that dates back to Pre-Migration Earth. There's no legal power behind it. Simply being a ship captain doesn't grant me that power."

Niven's expression sank and his skin took an unhealthy pallor at the captain's words. From his expression, this was definitely not part of the plan. And there was no backup. Gripping his whiskey tighter, his shoulders rose and fell in time with his quickening breaths. If Liam was right, it looked like Niven might break down given the right push.

"However, I do have that power. I always liked that old tradition and I hoped I might get the chance to use it someday."

Niven perked up. His eyes shimmered with unshed tears. "Really? You'll do it?"

"I'd be happy to."

Niven jumped up laughing—in near hysterics. He almost spilled his drink as he set it down on the desk, grabbed the captain's hand, and shook it like a madman. "Oh God! Thank you! Thank you!" He spun around and grabbed Liam by the shoulders, their faces centimeters apart.

"Liam! I'm getting married!"

"Not if you don't ask him first!" Liam laughed. Niven's enthusiasm was impossible not to mimic.

"Oh shit! You're right!" The surprise had yet to fade in Niven's face, mixed with an irrepressible joy. "I have to go!" He spun to the captain. "I'll talk to you soon!" In a flash, the eager man flew out of the room. Once the door slid shut, Danverse and Liam exploded, howling delight reverberating off the walls. Liam wiped his eyes with the back of his hand. Laughing so hard, he was almost in tears. Once they had calmed down to intermittent chuckles, Liam was able to breathe enough to speak.

"Did you see the look on his face when you told him the tradition had no legal power?"

A loud guffaw tore out of Danverse. "You'd swear I pistol whipped his puppy."

Liam let out an uncontrolled snort as he tried to hold back a fresh bout of laughter. "Why did you tell him that?"

"To make him sweat a little. I wanted him to work for it."

"I thought he was going to puke, he was so upset."

Danverse picked up Niven's discarded drink and split it between their glasses. "I had to have a little bit of fun under the circumstances."

"What circumstances?"

"Gamin pulled me aside during the dinner service last night and asked me for the same thing."

"Seriously? Gamin's going to propose to Niven tonight?" Liam's eyes were wide in delighted surprise.

Danverse shrugged with a grin. "It looks like they're going to propose to each other."

THREE YEARS, TWO MONTHS AGO

Everyone was dressed in what passed as his finest. On the *Santa Claus*, there wasn't a high need for fashion beyond the odd piece of off-hours fetish gear, but the men made do to the best of their ability. Even with this batch of roughnecks and hypermasculine males, there was an air of excitement and giddiness to be found amongst the men. No one had ever been married before on the ship.

There were few places to comfortably house the entire crew at once. The recreation rooms were a possibility. The observation deck could do so, but it was decided its structure and format would be an obstacle. Therefore, the mess hall was chosen. The venue held a dual reason for being used. It was, after all, where they had met.

The tables and chairs had been moved aside to make room for everyone to stand and watch. Captain Danverse looked impeccable at the front in his Marine dress uniform, flanked on either side by Niven and Gamin. Neither one held back their nervous smiles. They lit the room with an expectant vibration. Everyone in this little space-town community looked eager to share this event. Liam stood as Niven's attendant, while Thomas, the cook, stood with Gamin.

A voice shouted out from the crowd. "Who's the bride?"

The hall erupted in a torrent of laughter. Gamin saluted with his middle finger in the voice's direction.

Danverse's face curled into a snarl. "Shut the fuck up! This is a beautiful moment here, you little bitches."

The hilarity faded, with adolescent snickers here and there, until order was once again restored. Crew members' glances skittered back and forth amongst themselves, their mouths clamped tight to prevent a new chorus from escaping. Danverse looked awfully smug once it was clear he could proceed without interruption, the usual expression whenever his authority was established.

It was time to begin and Danverse's commanding voice filled the hall. "We are gathered here today to witness the union of Niven Anders and Gamin Wells. Two lives within the *Santa Claus* are about to become one in marriage. Is there anyone present who objects to this union?"

Danverse rolled a warning glare from one end of the crew to the other. When no one said a word, he continued:

"All of us in one way or another look for that person who completes us. We look for those people in strangers. We look for those people in our friends. We look for those people in our beds. Sometimes, the search consumes us, because it often seems an unreachable goal. Sometimes, it seems so impossible we simply give up.

"But if you're fortunate enough to find that other half of your soul, If the fates are kind and bring you both together, You must allow yourself to take in what they have to offer, And be prepared to return that in kind. Because it is a precious gift, and it must never be squandered.

"Never go to sleep angry. Always tell him you love him at least once a day. Find ways to make his life easier, and accept his attempts to do the same. Forge a bond between you that gathers the whole family, blood or adopted, and make love like you're learning each other for the very first time. Realize that you are not only marrying the right partner, you are being the right partner."

Liam watched the captain, entranced by his eloquence as each line was delivered with unerring sincerity. Captain Danverse was his best friend and they had spent countless nights together as friends and more, but he never imagined the alpha male capable of such subtle passion.

"Join hands and repeat after me: I take you...to be my partner. To have and to hold from this day forward. In sickness, in health, for better, for worse, I promise to be everything you've ever needed, and look forward to spending the rest of our lives making each other happy. I will love you forever until death do us part."

"Niven, do you take Gamin to be your lawfully wedded husband?"

"I do."

"Gamin, do you take Niven to be your lawfully wedded husband?"

"I do."

"May we have the rings please?" Each man's attendant produced a ring.

"These rings represent infinity and love never-ending. May it always be a token of your love and respect. Place the ring on each other's left hand and repeat after me:

"I...take you...to be my lawfully wedded husband."

The crowd followed with bated breath as both men played their parts with unsteady voices, hands bearing soft tremors, and sniffling between phrases. Once complete, they held hands adorned with matching platinum rings, staring into one another's eyes.

Danverse grinned from ear to ear. "And now by the powers vested in me, I pronounce you...husbands for life."

Gamin nearly lifted Niven off the ground with his kiss while every witness roared his approval in celebration.

THREE YEARS, ONE MONTH AGO

"Tell me why I have to be the one doing this again?"

Niven slid his hands into the makeshift gloves ending at the form-fitting sleeves. While zipping up the bodysuit made of reinforced flexible armor over his chest, Liam fitted the helmet over his head. The faceplate clicked into place as the suit locked the seams with an automatic hiss. A few quick checks to the seals and Niven was ready to go on a spacewalk if he wanted.

Liam patted him on the shoulder. "Privileges of rank. Plus, I'm bigger than you, and I can still push you around. Besides, you're the best man for the job."

"I hate these suits. They ride up my ass and make me walk funny." Niven's voice came through nice and clear over the com wrapped around Liam's ear.

"Well, now something other than Gamin can do that for you."

A stifled laugh underscored Niven's reply. "That's not funny, Liam."

"Yes, it is, newlywed."

"Son of a bitch." Niven flipped a middle finger at Liam, something else he'd never done before marrying Gamin.

Liam smirked as he keyed in the code to open Cargo Bay One. The bays were the only doors that were opened without a DNA ID scan. The security chief was the only one with the code once the *Santa Claus* was en route. It was one of Liam's idiosyncrasies the captain put up with. It had worked well for them so far. Why change it?

The massive door slid wide to the sight of rows and rows of crates stacked through the endless room. These shipments were the livelihood of everyone on board the ship. Niven stepped inside as Liam slapped a handheld scanner into his palm.

"So what, specifically, am I doing here, Liam?"

"We received an anonymous com about a possible bioweapon in one of the crates. Your job is to scan the hold and identify any possible biohazard so we can determine if there's any truth to it."

"You know I left the military so I didn't have to do this kind of shit anymore."

"Quit your bitching. You can take a spacewalk in that suit. You're perfectly safe."

"Mrs. Claus. Please seal the environment in Cargo Bay One from the rest of the ship for possible contagion." Liam tapped the control console and the door slid closed, its lock loud and solid. A small window centered in the door provided the only natural visual into the bay. In the background, Liam heard the mechanical shifting behind the walls as the protocols activated, segregating the large room.

"Environmental safety protocols are in effect, Sergeant Jacks," Mrs. Claus said.

Niven scanned crates one by one. "Why can't Mrs. Claus do this?"

"She already tried and came up empty, but a lot of the crates she can't get a clean scan of. The handheld is just a precaution."

"So I'm probably in this ass-riding suit for no reason then."

Liam chuckled. "With any luck, yes. Don't worry, though. I'm here with you all the way. I promised Gamin I'd look after you."

"I feel safer already."

From his vantage point at the little window, Liam watched Niven scan from crate to crate, row to row. It was a monotonous job, but it was necessary, even if absolutely nothing came of it. In all likelihood, the message was a hoax; it happened from time to time. But it didn't mean Liam didn't take it seriously.

"How's married life been treating you? Since you two have relegated your sex lives to your quarters, I hardly see you anymore."

"Oh fuck you, Liam." Niven's voice was filled with humor. "As to your question, it's been good. Best thing I ever did with my life was marry Gamin. The second thing was come on board the *Santa Claus*."

"Glad to hear Gamin came first."

"How could he not?" The smile on Niven's face was practically audible. He lit up like a nova at the mere mention of his husband. As much as it warmed Liam's heart, it pinched it as well. Pure yearning welled up witnessing their happiness. The ache wasn't for either Niven or Gamin. No, it was for what they had found and forged together, a union that took away the darkness—a darkness Liam continued to live with since the war.

"What the hell is this?" Niven's voice took an odd tone.

"Did you find a trace of biohazard?"

"No." Niven's speech became all too urgent. "Why is this crate shielded?"

He tore crates down from the pile at a reckless pace, ignoring the potential for damage. He unearthed a blue container, being too impatient, yet too careful, for Liam's comfort. Niven adjusted his scanner and took another reading.

"That can't be right. I need to get this open."

"Niven, did you find the bioweapon?"

Without answering, Niven tore open the crate and scanned its interior. "Oh fuck, Liam."

"What is it?"

"It's not a bioweapon." An edge of panic laced his voice. "It's a nuke."

"What? Is it live?"

Liam heard Niven's quickening breaths over his com. "Yeah. It's live. It's a micro-nuke, but it's still strong enough to take out the ship and us with it." Niven made desperate calculations on his scanner and fixed his attention to its readout.

"Can you disarm it?"

Niven tossed his scanner to the floor, cautiously reached into the crate, and drew out the object. The small mass of homemade tech fit into the palm of his hand, and Niven carried it like the finest crystal. How something so small could be so destructive always baffled Liam. Body stiff and cautious, Niven edged toward the rear of the bay.

"No." Niven spoke softly as if the volume held its own dangerous weight. "There isn't time. I'm dumping this bitch out the airlock. Get this boat moving, Liam."

Liam tapped the com at his ear. "This is Sergeant Jacks to the bridge. We have an emergency! Go to full throttle. Push us as fast as she can go."

"What's the emergency?"

"Don't ask! Just do it!"

The ship lurched under Liam's feet as it launched itself to full speed. He gasped when the shift caused Niven to stumble, but he caught himself and continued. Pressing himself to the bulkhead, Liam's eyes were fixed at the small window.

"Talk to me, Niven. How much time do we have?"

Niven's breathing was rapid and ragged. "Don't ask. Just keep us moving forward."

Liam's pulse was louder in his ears than the *Santa Claus*'s stressed engines. Icy sweat formed a line down his spine. Refusing to blink, he followed Niven as the outer airlock opened, he inched his way inside, and the door slid shut.

"Okay. I'm cycling the airlock. Come on. Faster, you bitch."

"Stay with me. You can do this, Niven." Even the few seconds it took for the airlock to void the atmosphere seemed an eternity they didn't have.

Niven whispered, his breath racing. "Opening the outer airlock. Out she goes."

A sudden flash of blinding light and a violent quake ripped through the hallway. Liam was thrown from the door, slamming against the opposite wall and to the floor. Alarms sounded as large emergency blast doors closed off the hallway on either side of him.

Mrs. Claus began her announcement with her calm, synthetic voice. "Emergency. Structural breach at Cargo Bay One airlock. Life support emergency protocols deployed."

Liam grabbed his com off the floor, wrapped it around his ear, and scrambled back to the cargo bay door, ignoring the burning ache from hitting the wall. The door was automatically locked by Mrs. Claus. The com was alive with frantic messages.

Captain Danverse's was the loudest. "Liam! What the fuck was that? What's going on?"

Ignoring it, Liam pressed his face to the tiny window. He flattened his hands against the cold metal as if he could push the barrier aside with his bare strength. Niven wasn't visible. The inner airlock was still closed.

"*Niven! Can you hear me?*" His shouts tore at his throat. "*Niven!*"

Nothing. In frustration, he pounded the immovable door with both hands. Sharp spikes of pain traveled up his wrists.

Liam's voice was frantic and loud. Panic sat at the edges of his vision, threatening to blind him. Niven had to be all right. He had promised Gamin he'd always look out for him. It was the only option.

"Mrs. Claus! Give me the bio-status of Niven Anders!"

Mrs. Claus responded as calm as ever. "I'm sorry, Sergeant Jacks. Niven Anders is no longer on board the *Santa Claus.*"

"YOU DON'T HAVE to do this, Liam. I'm the captain. Let me do this."

It had taken almost an hour to isolate the cargo bay and power the safety protocols down before the emergency bulkheads opened. An hour to dwell on things that couldn't be undone, leaving Liam broken and shaking. Danverse placed a hand on Liam's arm, but he jerked away.

"No. Niven was my responsibility." Every syllable was quiet and choked. "I have to be the one to tell him."

It was clear Danverse thought otherwise, but Liam's pleas beat him down and he relented.

Liam was fragile sugar glass as he looked down the corridor at the mess hall. He might have been walking through the gates of hell the way the sickly heat rose into his chest. Crushing his lids closed, he swallowed down the urge to vomit as his shoulders shook with tremors. Cold sweat soaked his clothing, adding to the fear running its daggers under his skin.

With a commanding hand, Danverse gripped the back of Liam's neck. "You can do this, Liam." Pulling Liam close, he growled in Liam's ear. "You will focus and do this with some dignity. You have to. For Gamin's sake. It's going to be all right."

"It will never be all right again." Liam ground his teeth as a tear ran down his cheek.

Danverse gave Liam a firm shake. "Look at me, Liam."

Liam opened his swollen eyes to find himself looking directly into Danverse's. The captain was weathered from the incident as well but had far more self-control than Liam possessed. He appeared strong in spite of the shadows under his eyes, the only giveaway of his restrained emotions.

Danverse's words were soft huffs against Liam's cheek. "It kills me to see you hurting this badly. I want to help make things right."

"How can I ever live with myself after this? After everything I've ever done?"

"I'll help you. Like I always do." He squeezed the back of Liam's neck. "Once this is done, you find me tonight. I'll take care of you." Danverse drew in a pained, deep breath. "But it won't be like before. I'll take you to the end of your limits."

Danverse palmed the back of Liam's skull and turned his head so he paid attention. "Have I made myself clear, boy?"

"Yes, sir. Thank you, sir."

Danverse rubbed his thumb along the nape of Liam's neck. "Now go in there and perform your duty, Sergeant."

With a new determination, Liam wiped his face and squared his shoulders before finishing the walk into the mess hall. Danverse beside him, he found Gamin and five other crew members still inside. Gamin was serving drinks and tending to the men sitting huddled together. Damage control reports showed they were in the mess hall when the blast doors came down.

Liam was so impressed with the man who took care of the others before himself. No wonder Niven had been so taken with Gamin and why they were so happy together. It made him nauseous just thinking of what he was about to do. When Gamin caught sight of Danverse and Liam, he rose from his work.

"Captain. Liam. Is everything all right? Everyone's still a little shaken since the emergency bulkheads came down. Are we okay?" Gamin looked over Liam. "Liam, can I get you anything? You look awful."

"No, thank you, Gamin. We need to find a place to talk."

Gamin paused as his expression became wary. "Liam...where's Niven?"

"Can we go somewhere private?"

"*Where's Niven?*" Gamin's bellow filled the room with a sick undercurrent, and Liam hesitated. This was exactly what he didn't want. An audience only made the whole thing more difficult than it already was.

Danverse reached up and laid a supportive hand on Liam's shoulder. The subtle warmth made him stand up tall and take a deep centering inhale.

"There was a nuke on board." Liam had to swallow to continue. "Niven found it in the cargo hold. He carried it to the airlock and tossed it out the door. He saved us."

One of the other crew broke in. "Is that what set off the alarms?"

Liam nodded.

Gamin's teeth were locked together as he snarled, his words almost incomprehensible. "Where is my husband?"

Liam struggled not to look away. "The explosion took out the outer airlock. Niven was still inside." Liam paused to find the strength to steady the words. "We lost him. I'm so sorry, Gamin."

As the news sank in, Gamin seemed to age. Natural laugh lines became deep chasms of sorrow as his face threatened to flow like molten wax. His shoulders slumped, his eyes became glassy, and his stance unsteady. Liam reached out for him as the first tear fell.

"*No!*"

Liam wasn't expecting the crushing fist that spun his head as Gamin launched himself at the unprepared security chief. The second and third blows fell as they slammed into the floor.

"*Gamin, NO!*" Danverse's order seemed to go unheard.

"*It should have been you! It should have been you!*" Gamin wailed through his tears. Liam choked on the blood in his mouth as his head snapped left and right with each impact.

"Gamin! Let him go! That's an order!" The mess hall filled with the cries of the crew members as they tried to pry them apart.

"You fucking cocksucker! You promised to look after him! You promised!"

Bone crunched as he spit out blood in order to breathe. The vision in his left eye was gone and all he knew was explosive pain and Gamin's raging sobs. Blow after crushing blow rained on him, and Liam did nothing to defend himself. He simply held on. Gamin was right. If Gamin wanted to take it in payment, his life was a minor price for his failure.

Gradually, the strikes slowed and stopped. Gamin's tortured cries were the only thing Liam heard as the chef slumped on top of him, burying his face into Liam's bloodstained shirt.

"It should...should have been you..." Gamin's halting voice was barely understandable. Gripping Liam in desperation, Gamin's inhuman weeping refused to abate. Hands still attempted to separate them and Danverse called out to see if he was all right.

With his strength gone, Liam could only reach up and put his arms around the grieving man. The crew finally stepped back when Liam refused to let Gamin go. One by one, they turned away, appearing unable to bear the horror of the broken men lying on the floor.

Chapter Eight

A PALL OF silence cloaked the room. Erron sat unspeaking, his mouth slack. His collar was damp with the tears streaking down his face as Liam finished his telling of Niven's story. Silent, yet visibly disturbed, Liam seemed unable to meet anyone's eyes. Hadrian gripped his partner's shoulder in support. Liam reached up, covering Hadrian's hand with his own.

Erron had to clear his throat to continue. In the quiet, it seemed obtrusive and loud.

"Did they ever find out who did it?"

Liam nodded. "A man named Jerek Gedron. He applied to join the crew on one of our stops in Fahrhammer. Danverse rejected him because he kept doing things during the interview that made him look unstable." Liam closed his eyes and took a breath. "It looks like he was right."

"What happened to him?" Hadrian's soft-accented voice was a comforting whisper in the tense atmosphere.

"The authorities tracked him down without much effort. He was so crazed he left evidence of all sorts behind. They discovered his military medical history had a diagnosis of paranoid schizophrenia and repeated bouts of refusing treatment. He should have spent his days in a sanitarium, but possession of a nuke is an automatic life imprisonment in the cluster. He's in a prison medical ward back on Fahrhammer. I check on him every so often and make sure he can't be released."

"How?"

"I have a friend who works on the parole board. If I have any say, Gedron's never getting out."

Erron exhaled in relief as he wiped his forearm along his eyes. Catching the fiend was meager consolation for the damage he had inflicted. It hardly measured as balanced justice, but at least some kind of closure came from it. Even though Erron had never known Niven, his heart reached out for Gamin. He must have truly loved Niven if the mere mention of him could undo Gamin after this many years.

"Why the secrecy surrounding Niven?"

"When you live in space like we do, you accept there are certain risks that come along with it. But no one expected this. It sent a ripple of fear through the crew and we nearly lost a lot of them. Gamin wasn't able to cope with the guilt and the loss."

Hadrian's head tilted and his eyes focused as if he were reading words floating in the air. "You made a pact."

Liam nodded. "Yes, we did. Gamin was the one who always took care of us. More than just the food. He made men who the world had cast aside after the war wanted and useful again. He was family. When his world crashed, we took care of him. No mention of Niven. Locked access to his personnel file. We weren't able to erase him off the Link, but we added firewall redirect viruses to the public feed and made him inaccessible to anyone on the *Santa Claus*."

Erron's eyes widened in surprise. "And Gamin agreed to that?"

"It was his idea. Gamin didn't want to leave the ship. It was his only home. So we granted him a wish. He didn't want to remember."

"Did Gamin start drinking heavily after it happened?"

"I think so. He was hurting so bad. We weren't sure how to handle it. He refused help and denied everything no matter how many times we found the empty bottles. Eventually, after several months, it came to an end. Gamin became like himself again and the evidence of his drinking disappeared. It seemed like he stopped."

"Do you really believe that?"

"He cleaned himself up and got back to work like he always did. Life on board went back to normal. I don't know what set him off. When do you think he started doing anything out of the ordinary?"

The memory of waking up under Gamin ran through Erron's mind. "I don't know. Maybe about a month after I got on board."

"Can you think of anything that caused it?"

Erron was puzzled. Gamin had broken his sobriety the night before they woke up together. It was the whole reason it happened in the first place. What else could possibly have been so bad it triggered a relapse after he'd joined the crew? He knew he should know the answer, but it escaped him. Was Gamin missing his husband? The only thing Erron had seen truly upset Gamin was...him.

That couldn't be right. Erron couldn't be the cause. His presence on the *Santa Claus* could not be the cause.

"Please don't let that be the reason." His thoughts came out in an audible whisper.

Liam heard it. "I'm sorry?"

Erron froze in his seat. After everything divulged this evening, he was not prepared to share his own worries. Erron waved it off. "It's nothing. Don't listen to me right now."

"Did it help to find out about Niven?" Hadrian petted Liam's head as he squeezed his hand.

"I'm not sure." Erron raked his hand through his hair. "It answers some things but leaves me with more questions I'm not sure what to do with."

Liam stood, his broad frame edgy and shaken. He had yet to face anyone since the story finished and his twitching fingers were one more sign of his agitation. Dipping his head, he turned and tried to retreat past Hadrian to the bedroom. Before he could vanish, Hadrian grasped Liam's wrist and pulled him close. No words were spoken as the huge man allowed himself to be wrapped up in his smaller companion.

"I'm sorry for bringing up such painful memories, Sergeant." Guilt seeped into Erron's voice at an uncontrollable rate as he crept closer to the door. He needed to leave. Witnessing this made Erron's presence an intrusion.

Liam lifted his head from Hadrian's shoulder but refused to release him. "It was bound to happen eventually. I just happen to have a lot of bad memories to manage. It's not your fault. Don't beat yourself up over it."

Erron reached for the panel and opened the door. "I can't help it. It seems like every time I ask a serious question, I just end up hurting people."

THE OBSERVATION DECK continued to fascinate Erron. Over the last few months, it had been a place to meditate, if that was the right word. Barrus was right about how, within the close quarters of the ship, there were few areas outside of a crew member's room to find a private location. Erron gravitated there more often these days in his rare off time. The sheer vastness of outer space had a calming effect on him. It was all about perspective. No matter how overwhelming his problems appeared, they were insignificant in the scope of the endless vacuum.

A week had passed since Sergeant Jacks had told him about Niven Anders, and Erron had yet to understand how to process the information. Or even what to do with it. While he understood an important portion of Gamin's past, it escaped him as to whether it helped. If not, Erron had badgered his way into a piece of confidential knowledge. That didn't set well with him.

Things between them had been somewhat different since they came back from Datham. The scent of alcohol had been less prevalent on Gamin the last few days, but Erron wasn't sure whether to call it a positive sign or if Gamin's skills at hiding it were improving. He wanted to kick himself for not pressing the matter further when they were in port. Given how quickly he had caved during the conversation, Erron found it hard to believe he'd actually gotten through to Gamin. Asking the important questions was never easy, was it?

Erron sighed as he settled back into the chair and gazed out into the universe. With their new vantage point en route to Alpha Centauri, the stars continued to be unrecognizable. The brighter stars were planets, but which ones, he had no idea. He wished he'd paid closer attention to his astronomy lessons. Was one of those little peaks of light Alpha Centauri? Did he care about coming so close to home?

So much had changed in so little time. One moment Erron was happy, another moment homeless and alone, then one moment in the right place, utterly confused. Even as complicated as everything had become, he still knew he belonged there on board the *Santa Claus*.

Lately, he had found himself reminiscing over that little diner he'd had that awful breakfast in before joining the crew. He wasn't sure why. It certainly wasn't a wish to remember the food. Disgusting. He actually kept replaying the awful woman pretending to be a fortune-teller.

"You think you've lost the ability to love another, but you'll find it on board once again."

Skank. He'd fallen for an age-old sideshow trick. The humiliation still made Erron's cheeks prickle in heat every time he thought about it. She was no psi. From the diner regulars' laughter, it was probably common for her to take advantage of people desperate to find answers. She was just a con after a few credits to buy her cheap-ass breakfast. The worst part, in spite of her phony insight, she was partially right. He had lost the ability to truly love another man, and even now, he still couldn't.

Gamin knew what true love was. He'd found it in Niven. The needy, passionate connection poets and novelists dream about. How a man can obsess day and night over what the other person is thinking and feeling, and whether they feel the same. How when they're separated, the spirit rips with longing, making him die a little inside. Erron had that with Toby. How humiliating to find out Toby thought otherwise.

In a way, Erron envied Gamin. His time with Niven was short—far too short—but was more complete than all of Erron's lifetime experiences combined. By every account, in their all-too-brief romance, Gamin was happy enough its loss nearly butchered his soul apart. Erron's relationship with James and Barrus paled in comparison.

And that was just another problem, wasn't it?

Erron was so steadfast in his need to help Gamin, he was ignoring his own needs. James and Barrus were wonderful. They doted on Erron and showed him how to be wanted. God knows, it had been a foreign concept when he'd boarded. In fact, Erron felt more confident than he had in ages. The pair were amazing lovers and so much fun to be around. Wasn't that enough?

No. It wasn't.

Unless they were in bed next to him, he rarely woke thinking of them. When they weren't together, he didn't find himself pining over their absence. Shouldn't that be telling him something? Erron wasn't able to see the long-term with the three of them. He couldn't picture the future, and for him, it was a requirement. James and Barrus were never selfish in telling him how much they enjoyed Erron's company and he knew they wanted it to be something more serious and permanent.

When he'd first come to them, he was hurting so much. Getting involved with James and Barrus had been a good thing. It hadn't been long before his history with Toby stopped choking his memories and he believed he might move on. Because of them. But the distraction of two men was keeping him from finding the intimacy he needed. An intimacy Erron only saw with the concentration of a single partner.

Also, his involvement with them was a constant source of friction with Gamin. They had lost track of each other for so long, Gamin didn't look willing to risk a new separation. His protective streak was in full bloom, and Gamin didn't need any more triggers. If his drinking had any chance of recovery, his world needed stability. Connected as they were, before Erron could help Gamin, his own life needed cleaning up.

Stars or planets, whatever they were, twinkled in the blackness outside. It was far easier to manage a moment of clarity there, in the stoic dark, no matter how unpleasant. He fingered the armrest with one hand as he raked through his hair with the other. With an inspiration born from stray starlight, there was the obvious realization.

Gamin would always be far more important to him than James and Barrus.

"Damn." His quiet curse was for no one's ears in the empty room.

That was proof enough of what needed to be done. Rubbing both hands over his face, Erron's breath escaped him in a rush. He only hoped he had the strength to go through with it.

THREE MORE DAYS had passed, and Erron found himself in front of James and Barrus's quarters, waiting for them to appear. Remorse flooded his chest as he paced in a circle in front of the door. During those three days, Erron hadn't found the courage to speak.

He had even slept with them the night before. Why did it have to be so good? The three of them had taken turns with each other all night. He swore he still tasted the salt and sex. It was sweaty, distracting, hot, and left Erron morally soiled the next morning.

Erron had tried to broach the subject the previous night. It was too hard. The words stalled when flashbacks of the times he had hurt people, saying the wrong thing at the wrong time, came forward instead. James and Barrus were so concerned with how upset he became, and before he knew it, Erron had deflected his anxiety, escaping into mind-numbing, carnal pleasure. It was selfish indulgence and made him think he was using them. Erron cursed himself all day. How much easier his choices if he lacked a conscience like Toby. His ex had basically done the same to him and would have continued given the chance. That thought bolstered his resolve. It was time for Erron to make things right. Immediately.

James and Barrus rounded the corner and Erron's chest tightened in suspense. As soon as they saw him, both of their faces brightened. A wave of heat rose into Erron's face. Even with his newfound courage, this was still going to be difficult.

"We weren't expecting to see you." James's brief scan of Erron's expression dimmed his smile. "Is everything all right?"

A shudder traveled down Erron's spine. "I need to talk to you both."

"Well, let's go inside." Barrus reached for the door control, and Erron stopped his hand.

"Not inside." Eyeing the door, Erron remembered what had happened last night. "Out here will be fine."

Barrus pulled back, his brow flattened, an obvious suspicion in his stare. "Erron, what's going on?"

Erron nodded as he tried to order his thoughts. He had rehearsed this over and over for the last twelve hours. Now the moment was here, and all the effort turned to rubbish. Useless, incoherent words stammered out of his mouth, forcing him to start and stop several times.

"Hey, relax." James ran his fingers through the side of Erron's hair. The tender brushing along his scalp often put him at ease. James had been a quick study. "Nothing can be that planet-shattering. Take a breath and let it out slowly."

Erron felt his eyes swelling. This was so awful. The last thing he wanted to do was hurt them when they had been so good to him.

"I don't think I can keep seeing you both." The words were near whispers brimming with tears. "It's not right for me. And it's not fair to you both."

Barrus stilled, and James looked a little sad but controlled. When Erron lowered his head in shame, James raised it again and caught his eyes.

"Is that what last night was about?"

All Erron managed to do was nod. Chest pounding and sickeningly light-headed, he didn't trust his reaction aloud.

James shared a sad look with Barrus, then surrounded Erron with his arms. Barrus was right there as well, as always, shielding them.

"Erron, it's all right." Barrus's whisper puffed along Erron's temple. "We told you before there wasn't any pressure."

James gave Erron a little smile. "We also said that if things didn't work, we would never stop being your good friend."

Erron's eyes widened as he looked between them. He sniffed and took a stuttered breath. "You're both okay with this?"

James's shrug was subtle. "*Okay* is a bit strong of a word, but we understand. We wondered if something like this was going to happen. Barrus and I are observant people."

"Sometimes these things just run their course." Barrus gave him a thin smile. "Not every relationship has to end like yours and Toby's."

"You don't hate me then?" Erron's voice quivered.

James and Barrus tightened the embrace immediately. "Oh, Erron. We could never hate you. I won't say we're not disappointed, but don't ever think that."

Erron pulled back in wonder. James stroked his cheek while Barrus ran his firm hand down Erron's neck and back. How did he deserve these two men in the first place? It really was a shame he wasn't in love with them.

A wistful sigh shifted James's chest. "We always knew you'd ultimately only stay with someone you were in love with."

"I really do love you guys. I wish it was right for me to stay."

"You have to do what's right for you. We don't want it any other way."

Erron gave each man a crushing hug and kiss in turn. "I'm so sorry. Thank you so much for understanding."

"We'll come through it fine." James appeared disappointed but fine. "Now go on. I can smell you haven't showered since you finished your work shifts. You smell like sweat, lunch, and dinner."

Barrus chimed in. "Better get cleaned up before I throw you over my shoulder and take you there myself. That would kind of invalidate what just happened here."

Erron smiled as James spun him around and gave him a playful swat on his ass to get him moving. Rounding the corner, he headed toward his quarters to grab his gear and get cleaned up. A hasty sniff said James was right. He was ripe.

As Erron walked down the hall, the weight lifted from his chest. The conversation had gone better than he hoped. Not counting his meltdown, of course, but he wasn't thinking of that now. The grin graced his lips and made his cheeks ache. Breaking up with someone was never easy under the best of circumstances, but he was overwhelmed at the idea everything was right between them.

He stopped in his tracks just short of opening his door. Thumping his forehead with the heel of his hand, Erron growled at himself. Part of the plan this evening was to retrieve his favorite hat, the one he'd been wearing when he first stepped on board. It had been left in their quarters the night before and he needed to wear it to work tomorrow. Because he refused to wear one of those hair socks. No. With a bounce, he headed back the way he came.

Erron came around the corner to find James and Barrus still in the hallway. Barrus's strong arms surrounded James as he buried his face into Barrus's chest and shoulder.

"It's not fair." James's voice was partially muffled against his husband.

"I know, baby. But we can't make him stay."

"I don't want him to go, Barrus."

Barrus leaned back and raised James's chin with his finger. "Don't you want him to be happy?"

"Of course I do." James spoke through gritted teeth, his tone a mix of anger and frustration.

Barrus touched his forehead to James's. "We talked about it. We both saw it coming."

"I know. I just hoped that we'd find a way to make him happy with us."

Erron's spine chilled as Barrus replied so soft he almost missed it. "You really loved him too. Didn't you?"

"Just as much as you did."

Erron couldn't bring himself to move. Even in the middle of the hall, watching this happen was an intrusion of the highest order. But he was terrified to move and risk them noticing him, so he stayed silent as a new weight crushed his chest.

Fisting handfuls of Barrus's shirt, James closed his eyes, and his head dropped. "I didn't think I'd hurt this bad, Barrus."

"I'm so sorry, baby. If I thought it'd be like this, I wouldn't have let us get so attached." The growing coarseness of Barrus's speech belied the calm in his effort to soothe James.

Hard creases lined James's face as he burrowed into the sanctuary of his husband's chest with a hard gasp. "It's not fair."

"Don't worry, baby." Barrus spoke along his husband's temple. "I'll take care of you. I have a new vid we can watch, and I have some of those sweets you like so much. Let's go in and bury ourselves in bed. Just you and me. We don't have to come out until morning. I will always be there for you. I love you, James."

James's voice finally broke. "I love you too, Barrus."

Barrus sniffed hard and tightened his embrace before leading James back to their quarters. James didn't even look up as Barrus opened the door. As they stepped inside, Barrus glanced back and found Erron watching. Devastated, Erron's breath stopped as the door closed behind them with a grim finality.

THE BREAKFAST SHIFT dragged. Erron spent most of his time in the back doing prep work during the meal service while Gamin worked up front. It was probably a good thing. The monotonous activity helped distract him from the breakup the previous night and his unbridled remorse. He hadn't slept well either. Thankfully, Gamin didn't notice or was too polite to say anything. At least he showed up on time this morning. Erron really didn't need the additional stress on top of it.

Erron found himself watching Gamin more closely now. Not in a critical way, but somehow looking for the qualities that made him the single choice for Niven Anders. Gamin was a tall, broad-shouldered man with meaty limbs and extra padding around the waist like a powerlifter. He was considerate, playful, and warm, and would make any man an ideal husband.

Hopefully, someday Erron would find such qualities in a partner of his own. Even if he had only known it a short time, he envied Gamin for finding it.

When they ate together during the break, Erron noticed how much he liked the dark hair gracing Gamin's brawny forearms. The pleasant rumble of Gamin's voice was calming and made Erron's problems appear much smaller. As Gamin brought him a plate with a simple serving of the lunch menu, he felt cared for in a way that Toby never had. He even liked the scent of the man eating next to him.

Why couldn't he find that in one man for him?

The lunch service was more of the same drudgery, except Erron found himself serving at the buffet to the line of appreciative crew members. One by one, they came through. Erron's chest was tight, knowing eventually James and Barrus would arrive.

They showed up together as they did for every meal. This time with a plaintive stance and downcast eyes. Barrus knew Erron had witnessed them in the hallway, and by James's reaction, he knew as well. Their bawdy and exciting inner spark was turned down low. It curdled Erron to know he was the cause.

At that moment, Gamin walked through the kitchen door, carrying a tray of pasta to replace a near-empty pan in the buffet.

James cleared his throat as he spoke. "How are you doing, Erron?"

"I'm good. How are you guys?" Erron's response was difficult and stilted.

Barrus shrugged. "We're all right. We missed you at breakfast." His eyes shifted back and forth between the chef and cook.

"Gamin had me doing prep in the back."

Both men nodded as Erron served them both. They tried to be nonchalant, but Erron had come to know them too well in the past few months. No words were spoken. They simply pointed at their selections. Polite smiles were had by all, but they were forced and impatient. It was just like their mutual friends Toby and Erron shared after the breakup. He remembered the way they had spoken to each other in false platitudes because it was easier than being honest. It was too much like the painful past. From the corner of his eye, Erron noticed Gamin watching the cold interaction.

"We'll talk to you later, Erron." James nodded in Erron's direction while leading Barrus to a table on the far side of the mess hall. They sat at the end across from each other, Barrus looking up one last time at Erron before engrossing himself in his meal.

Separating from James and Barrus was the right thing to do, but why did it have to be so awful? The sigh that escaped Erron was louder than he expected.

Gamin placed a hand along Erron's lower back. "Is everything all right between you three?"

"There is no 'we three' anymore." Erron found himself leaning into the heat of Gamin's hand. It was the only thing offering solace.

"When did this happen?"

"Last night."

Gamin's brow creased as his soothing touch dragged up and down. "What happened?"

I stabbed two men who loved me in the heart just like Toby did. Images of James and Barrus in the hallway and the words they spoke after he broke with them rose to the front of his mind.

Erron breathed deep and swallowed down the tear that almost escaped him. "I...I don't want to talk about it."

Gamin's hand stilled as Erron squeezed his eyes closed to get his emotions under control.

When he opened his eyes again, Gamin looked livid. Why? Erron was at a complete loss. Gamin untied his apron and whipped it to the ground, stepping on the stained fabric as he stalked around the buffet line.

Was Gamin angry with him? He knew Gamin had never completely approved of his relationship with James and Barrus but didn't expect him to be angry over it coming to an end. Why wasn't he relieved? He hadn't been thrilled over their relationship from the start. Erron was lost in his thoughts until he realized Gamin was marching through the mess hall in a direct line to James and Barrus.

Without warning, Gamin raised his large boot and stomped it into Barrus's seated chest, sending him smashing backward into the floor and wall. The sound of chairs crashing along the floor startled Erron. No one had the chance to react as Gamin spun on James, grabbing him by the shirt. Gamin's face was a mask of rage as he punched James solid in the face. Nearby crew members scrambled to get out of the way.

Erron shouted as he rounded the counter. "Gamin! No!" As Gamin planted a second blow to James's face, Erron rushed forward only to be stopped by Carson.

"Don't, Erron." Carson struggled to hold Erron back. "They have to get this out. It's been coming for a while."

"What do you mean, 'coming for a while'?"

Carson shot Erron a piercing look, his brow arched. "Are you kidding? Don't you know who they're fighting over?"

Everything was so wrong. Erron's chest was beating so hard, it was making his head swim. Hearing the story of Gamin's attack on Liam did not prepare him for this kind of fight. Gamin dropped James and, before Barrus got up again, kicked him in the side so hard it lifted him off the ground. The winded grunt was sickening. Faster than Erron thought possible, Gamin whirled, snatched James from the ground, and placed him in a painful headlock.

"I fucking knew this would happen." Gamin's temper warped his voice. Choking, James sputtered and clawed at Gamin's arm.

"As soon as you two pieces of shit got a hold of Erron, I knew you'd fuck him over." Gamin's fury frightened Erron more than the violence in front of him. Holding his side, Barrus tried to roll over, but Gamin pinned Barrus to the floor by his throat, using his big foot. With a rough shove, he heaved James into a group of chairs, upending a table. The harsh clash echoed through the hall.

Erron shouted for Gamin to stop, but the words slurred and garbled. The dizziness was back and his face felt numb. When he tried to figure out what was wrong, his arm refused to lift.

"Gamin, we didn't break up with Erron." James grunted and winced as he shoved a chair aside and struggled to rise. A line of blood ran down from his hairline to accompany the swelling already showing in his face. He slipped once and had to try again before he was steady enough to stand.

"Don't fucking lie to me." It was obvious Gamin didn't believe a word.

Barrus gasped, his words barely came out under the pressure of Gamin's boot. "He dumped us."

"Why would he do that?"

James half limped, inching his way closer to Gamin. "Because he's in love with you, you fat bastard!"

At the utterance, Erron froze. The shock built and formed a spike of thorns that drilled through Erron's skull. He slumped into Carson's arms, his legs refusing to hold him and his vision was dimming on his left side. What was that coppery taste? His breathing and heartbeat went erratic and everything stopped.

Gamin's anger stuttered long enough for James to smash a fist across his nose. The crunch of bone was audible. Another slice of agony rolled behind Erron's eyes and the dizziness turned into full-blown vertigo. It was difficult to realize he wasn't holding himself up anymore.

Carson pierced through the haze. "Erron? Erron, you're bleeding. Can you hear me?" He sounded so far away, but he knew somehow the medic was right there supporting his body. The room whirled as Erron's head rolled back of its own accord.

Carson hovered over him. Erron thought he was lying on the floor, but the burning in his head was so bad he wasn't sure. The world had grown so hollow. Carson was trying to get his attention. Erron tried over and over to speak, to scream, to do anything for himself. He could hear. He could see, but nothing was working.

"Mrs. Claus! Get Dr. Bosch! Medical emergency to the mess hall!" Carson's worried call filled the room. "Erron Murfin is down! External cranial bleeding from the ears and nose and possible massive hemorrhagic stroke." Someone's fingers touched along Erron's neck. "His pulse is weakening! Hurry up! I'm losing him!!"

All Erron heard were the shouts of Gamin, James, and Barrus as his world blurred and darkened into nothing.

Chapter Nine

"...CAN YOU HEAR me?"

The darkness was lifting, leaving Erron swimming in molasses. Sharp, bright lights waved back and forth, search beacons across his field of vision. Electronic chimes in the distance had a pattern sounding suspiciously like a heartbeat. Erron recognized the bedside timbre of Dr. Bosch's voice. It did nothing to ease the anxiety growing inside him. He was in sick bay.

"Erron? Can you hear me?" Someone snapped their fingers directly above Erron's face.

"His eyes are moving." The gruff voice could only belong to Carson. Memories solidified and lost their quicksilver qualities. The miscommunication. The brawl. Carson holding him while calling for a medical emergency. Fading away into nothing. Erron thanked the stars Carson had been in the mess hall.

Staring at the ceiling, Erron found Carson and Dr. Bosch hovering over him with earnest faces. Both carried handheld scanners, looking between the screens and Erron as they passed them over his body. Flashes of light filtered in from the edge of his vision, but when he tried to turn his head to see them, nothing happened.

"Blink for me, Erron." Dr. Bosch snapped his fingers again. "Once for yes. Twice for no."

Blink. It was difficult, but Erron managed it.

"Can you speak?"

The strangled sound startled Erron. Was that him? Why didn't it sound right? *No, no, no.* Quick, panicked breaths pushed past his lips as a single tear spilled out of the corner of his eye.

Blink. Blink.

"Scan shows auditory and optical functions were unaffected." Carson showed the doctor his readout.

Dr. Bosch agreed with a gesture. "Good. You've had a massive stroke, Erron. I believe it was caused by an extremely rare side effect of the medication I had you on for the artificial gravity symptoms. It only presents itself by a rise in blood pressure and random dizzy spells. The final trigger is usually a high-stress situation. I'd guess what I heard happened in the mess hall qualifies."

Blink.

"You've been having dizzy spells but ignored them, figuring they would just go away. Am I correct?"

Blink.

Carson leaned close with a raised finger in front of Erron's face. "Follow my finger."

Erron focused on the digit as it slowly slid left and right.

"Good, Erron."

"I'm guessing you didn't read the info packet I messaged you that explained this?"

Blink. Blink.

"You do have a habit of drowning people in information with your coms, Doc." Carson caught Erron's attention again. "Raise your right hand, Erron. Now your left."

Dr. Bosch's brow flattened. "The captain has said as much."

"Squeeze my hand, Erron." Carson shared a look with the doctor and shook his head. The move was so minute Erron knew the medic was trying to hide it.

"This is as much my fault as anyone's, Erron. I should have gone over the possibilities in more detail, but didn't want to frighten you." Bosch sighed. "Now look where we are.

"You're no longer in danger of another stroke, but there's been some damage. Since you're awake, Carson is running some physical tests while we're scanning you to determine the extent. Some of it can't be repaired directly, gray matter doesn't respond reliably to regenerators, so I need to put in some neural implants to bypass the damaged brain cells and hopefully get you back somewhere closer to normal. Your motor skills have been extremely compromised. I can't tell you you'll be exactly like new. But if I don't do this, in all likelihood you'll be in this bed for the rest of your life."

Terror stabbed Erron in the chest. A torrent of tears overflowed his eyes and wet his temples while his cries were nothing more than incoherent whimpers squeezing out of his useless flesh. Dr. Bosch's lips tightened with a grimace. His professional veneer was beginning to peel. Erron had never seen the doctor show any emotion other than annoyance with his patients. The display terrified him.

"It is a surgical procedure, but I can't do this without your consent. Do I have your permission to continue?"

Blink.

"Good boy." A relieved smile graced the doctor. Eyes misty, he brushed a lock of hair off Erron's forehead. "I'll take good care of you, Erron. I promise."

"I THOUGHT YOU might like to see a familiar face." Liam stepped forward and sat along the edge of Erron's bed. "Bosch said it was okay for you to have a visitor."

From his office on the other side of the room, Dr. Bosch called across the infirmary. "A short visit." The man was engrossed in his work, visible through the open double doors, but he was well aware of his charge in bed.

Erron's words were a struggle. "You're...the first." Two days had passed since the fight in the mess hall and he had only been awake a few hours since the surgery. The monitors' soft chirping of his vitals was a constant buzz he was quickly learning to tune out. Lying down in his bed didn't leave Erron with a very good view, but he appreciated the presence of someone not involved with the medical staff.

With a clumsy hand, Erron pushed the hair down over his left ear, the side of his hand serving as a blunt brush since his fingertips refused to cooperate. His arm awkwardly swayed as it barely responded to his command. Erron touched the five small pieces of tech forming a crescent around his ear, the only physical evidence of his procedure. They served as data ports for the neural implants teaching his body to function again.

Liam didn't react to Erron's clumsy move. "Only because the others aren't allowed. Gamin, James, and Barrus are restricted to quarters and essential duties. They're not allowed anywhere near sick bay. Mrs. Claus is even monitoring their constant locations. The captain isn't very tolerant of fights among the crew, so he's more than a little pissed. Plus, they've been annoying the hell out of me for an update. They're a little cranky since the pain meds have been kept to a minimum for them."

Erron gave the sergeant a perplexed stare.

"Sorry, Erron. I keep forgetting you're out of the link. They busted each other up pretty well. Between the broken noses, ribs, and cheekbones, the three of them are healed up, but not completely. A little reminder from the captain.

"It's actually a good thing. Punishment used to be a night at the captain's mercy, which is not for the faint of heart. He's found new means of enforcement. He doesn't fuck the crew anymore since he finally connected with his partner, Mac."

Another confused glance curled Erron's brow.

"Mac? Head tech? Short, stocky youngster with a dirty sense of humor."

Erron's face must have shown Liam he remembered. His head was still a bit murky, and his condition dug at his confidence.

Erron faced away from Liam. "I don't want...them here, Liam. I don't...want them to see...me like this."

"Are you sure?"

Of course not. Erron's first word when he woke after surgery was Gamin's name. A stranger in his own body, he'd give anything for Gamin's supportive embrace, but he wasn't willing to bear pity from him. And when he finally witnessed Erron's state of mind and health, he'd get more of it than he could stomach. No. The potential horror and pain in Gamin's eyes would be far too much for Erron to stand. The same held for James and Barrus, no matter how hard they pleaded. He'd hurt them enough for an eternity.

"I can't...even feed myself, Liam. Or much of...anything else." Even speaking was strained, his voice pausing at odd moments. The words were there, but he choked on them and spit them out forcefully without intending to. While he was thankful to regain the power of speech, such as it was, the rest of his body was running far behind in comparison.

"Do you think you'd be up for a few questions? I'd like to hear from you what happened."

"Okay. They say I need...the practice to reteach...me." Erron shrugged. Or at least tried to. His shoulders didn't really move much when he tried. Thankfully, Liam wasn't repulsed or treating him differently. Erron wasn't sure he could face that from anyone at the moment. It was too upsetting. He had enough to punish himself over for several lifetimes.

"What set Gamin off?" Liam reached for a water cup complete with sipping straw from the bedside table. Erron accepted when Liam presented it with a questioning nod. Taking a sip was an effort, but a successful effort. A small victory.

"I told him...that James, Barrus...and I broke up."

Liam raised an eyebrow as he returned the cup to its resting space. "James and Barrus both said you broke it off with them. Why would Gamin care?"

"He mis...understood. He thought they...dumped me."

The sergeant's face brightened in understanding. It was as if the last piece of a puzzle clicked into place, finally complete. "So he got pissed and took it out on them. Defending your honor and all." Liam smirked.

Erron smiled a little bit in return. Finding the urge encouraged him in some small way. "Such as...it is." The smile, however, was fleeting. "I didn't realize...at first. Then the fight...started. I tried to...stop it, but...this happened... first." He raised and dropped his arms to the bed like dead weight to illustrate.

He felt so helpless. In spite of the drama that had been stirring around him, Erron was prepared to work through it. Now, he lay in bed, his body a stranger, wondering if he'd ever be like himself again.

"Can you raise...me up? Lying...down makes me feel...like a cripple."

Liam hopped off the bed and tapped the panel along the side. With barely a sound, the bed flexed upward, and it wasn't long before Erron was sitting upright. Trying not to appear strained, he placed his hands in his lap so they didn't look like broken appendages.

"You found...the controls awfully...fast."

Liam ducked his head, his voice melancholy. "I've been in this bed before." He sat back on the edge of the bed, reminding Erron of how he reacted to telling Niven's story.

"When?"

"About four or five months ago. We were boarded. That had never happened before. I took a gunshot wound to the chest." Liam's hand rose, his fingers unconsciously grazing a circle over the wide muscle.

Erron's eyes went wide in shock. "How? What...did you do?" How had he not heard about this? Was this another secret the crew held close to themselves?

"You're not going to be here long enough to tell that story, Liam," Dr. Bosch called out.

Liam looked back to the office and nodded. The doctor's tone made it clear Liam's visit was coming to a close. Erron was a little saddened by it but understood. Even this short round of conversation was exhausting. If he allowed it, the weakness would drag him back to sleep. He was a fraction of himself. Liam turned back and placed a warm hand on Erron's shoulder, his gentle grin an unexpected beacon.

Erron raised his voice for Dr. Bosch's benefit. "I can see...privacy's...a luxury...I can't afford."

"In my sick bay, there's no such thing." Dr. Bosch was back to his normal temperament, monitoring and controlling every aspect of Erron's recovery like some infirmary emperor. His head never rose up from reading the screen, but he made it obvious sick bay was his domain.

Liam chuckled. "Short version: I got shot. Doc Bosch took care of me. I got better. So will you."

"WHAT IS THIS, Hadrian?"

"It's paper."

"I can see that. What...are you doing with it?" Erron's speech had become significantly stronger in the past three days. The pauses were less frequent, but it still bothered him. Walking unaided without injuring himself was beyond his current skills, so Erron found his current residence in sick bay. He sat upright in bed, facing Hadrian who sat cross-legged on the opposite end. Several squares of paper, fifteen centimeters by fifteen centimeters, sat on a metal tray lying on the mattress between them.

"It's an exercise." Hadrian picked up a single sheet and carefully folded it.

Erron wasn't sure what kind of exercise Hadrian required. The man was gorgeous and fucking perfect. Everything he wore showed off his body and accented his magnetism. Was it on purpose, or was he unconscious of the effect he had on others? Graced with olive skin and the brightest blue eyes Erron had ever seen, which might hypnotize the most devoted celibate. Muscles in his arms flexed as he worked. The top buttons open down Hadrian's sleeveless shirt gave Erron a lovely view. The metal band on Hadrian's left arm always intrigued Erron, but he was far too intimidated to ask why the tattoo on his shoulder disappeared underneath it without reappearing down his arm like it should. He wondered if Hadrian realized how provocative his presence was.

"Hadrian, is that tray from the mess hall?"

"Hush, Erron."

For all his size and power, Hadrian folded the square into itself, forming diamonds and triangles. Deft fingers worked without rushing, entrancing Erron with the deliberate yet elegant movements. Scant minutes passed before Hadrian placed a small miniature dragon on Erron's seated thigh. Tiny feet jutted from the serpentine body, its wings a lattice of geometric perfection.

"That's amazing," Erron whispered, awestruck. A deep furrow formed between his brows as he looked at the remaining slips of paper. "I can't...make that."

Hadrian placed a small stack of sheets on the tray. "I would hope not. I needed almost a month to learn how to fold that form without instructions in front of me. It is quite complicated."

Erron's eyes darkened. "Then why show it to me? That...seems a little unfair."

"To show you what is possible."

With his index finger, Hadrian slid a single sheet from the group over to Erron's side of the tray. Staring at the little square, a small glaze of unease washed over him. Hadrian didn't really expect him to do something like that, did he? He nearly balked aloud as Hadrian pulled a sheet for himself.

With an instructor's tone, Hadrian spoke. "Do what I do." Picking up one corner, he folded the square into a perfect triangle and smoothed the crease with the pad of his finger. Hadrian gazed up at him with his ice blue eyes, signaling Erron's turn.

Erron frowned but relented. He labored to pick up the sheet of paper, let alone fold it over. Crude movements folded over the square, but the result was far less than perfect and the seam was crushed rather than creased. He stared at the mangled piece of paper, his eyes welling.

"I don't...think I can do this." Erron groaned under a shaky exhale.

Hadrian reached over and placed his hands over Erron's. With patient care, he guided Erron's hands through the motions for the simple fold. Once complete, Hadrian went back to his own and performed the next step.

"You are impatient." Hadrian guided Erron through the second movement. "From what Dr. Bosch has told me, it was not so long ago that the technology to perform the neural implants did not exist. It would have taken you months, if not years—or at all—to regain what you have in less than a week. Your progress has been exemplary."

Erron growled in frustration. "Easy for you to say. Your body never...betrayed you like this."

Hadrian stopped and stared. His visage was so stoic, Erron couldn't tell if he was sad, angry, or 100 percent apathetic. Odd silence filled the sick bay as he waited to see if Hadrian had anything to say.

"Before I came on board, I lived my life as a slave. With a single phrase, my...owners tortured me like a rabid dog to keep me in line and did so often. There was nothing I could do while I writhed in agony on the floor and wet myself.

"Eventually, I was freed, but not before I lost my arm defending Liam. Burned off by a particle weapon during our escape." Hadrian raised his left arm. Erron's gaze ran up the muscled limb, landing on the armband lying below the deltoid. The realization blossomed for Erron.

"Lost your arm? That's why the tattoo...disappears under the armband, isn't it? It's artificial?"

Hadrian gave a nod, a single move of grace. "It took a month of adjustments and physical therapy to regain the use of my hand. Having a portion of my body disconnected from me was very difficult. Even to this day, the sensations are somewhat alien, but I have grown accustomed to it. The origami was part of that process. So I know a little of what I am speaking of."

"Why the origami?"

Pausing, Hadrian's head tilted as he looked off in contemplation, impossibly handsome in reflection. "Because it is simple and elegant and precise. Making paper animals always left me with a sense of peace when my life was filled with abuse and violence. It centered me."

Erron didn't know how to respond, so he went back to the task at hand. Hadrian continued each step and then led Erron through his turn. Back and forth they went, Erron's forehead shiny in concentration until a tiny paper rabbit sat on the tray before him.

"I still can't do...that without your help." Erron didn't embrace the idea of satisfaction. "My body doesn't do much of what I want these days. I don't feel particularly...human right now."

"Is that why you refuse to see Gamin, James, or Barrus?"

"I don't want their pity. Besides, they...must hate me. I've done so much damage to them."

"Hate is not what I gather from them. Their frustration at being kept from you is practically audible across the ship. People who love you forgive and forget, Erron."

Erron's face twisted in anger. "They'll just feel sorry...for me! They'll have that look on their faces that...reminds me of what I'll never be again." Anger bled out of Erron with a sudden breath, choked down by a fear he hadn't uttered until now. "I can't get...out of this bed or even walk without someone's...help. Dr. Bosch doesn't know if I'll ever be back to normal again."

Hadrian rolled forward and embraced Erron even as the tears fell. It was the first real hug he'd had since arriving in sick bay. Hadrian was strong, but it was nothing like the way Gamin's arms enveloped him. A small part of him wished he'd never refused to see the three men, but he simply didn't want Gamin seeing him in this state. He wished hard to be the man he once had been.

As they pulled away, Hadrian cupped Erron's face in his hands. Ice blue eyes glinting in the artificial light, Hadrian smiled back at him in comfort, not in pity. Erron followed the path of Hadrian's left thumb as it wiped away the moisture pooling under his eye. The hand might have been artificial, but felt real enough. If Hadrian hadn't said anything, Erron might never have noticed.

"You are correct, Erron. There are no promises here. The only guarantee I have is that if you do not try, you will almost certainly fail."

"Okay." Erron swallowed hard, seeking to compose himself. "Let's...try again."

Chapter Ten

"YOUR PROGRESS HAS been incredible." A tone of awe underscored Dr. Bosch's voice as he ran his portable scanner over the ports around Erron's ear. It passed over without touching but gave off a meager hum, the vibration itching the surrounding bone. Somehow, Erron managed to hold still, seated on the sick-bay bed he despised.

"How much more will I get back?"

"The nano-filaments have fully integrated themselves through your brain. Your recovery will likely be in more gradual steps rather than the huge jumps you've experienced over the last two weeks."

"But I'm still not normal." Erron wished he shared the doctor's enthusiasm, but dressing himself that morning had been another humiliating experience.

Dr. Bosch sighed. "Erron, your stroke was nearly catastrophic. I wasn't sure how much you'd regain even with the nanotech. The chance of success was slim, but we knew there wasn't any choice. You're fortunate not to be trapped inside your body for the rest of your life."

"I'm still trapped."

"Your speech is nearly restored, as well as much of your motor function." Dr. Bosch set down his scanner and focused on the nearby monitor displaying a new set of incomprehensible medical stats.

"Much...but not all." Erron looked down at his hands and tried to touch his thumb to each of his fingers. The effort was clumsy and required a great deal of concentration. It was true. Two weeks ago, this had been impossible. He should have been happy, but he only felt bitter disappointment. Hope did not have the power to cure everything. Erron railed at the news as he held back the urge to scream and cry.

"Considering your condition when you arrived in sick bay, I'd say you should be proud to get this far."

"But I'm still a cripple."

"Just because your progress has plateaued is no reason to mean it's ended."

"It's not guaranteed to continue, though, either, is it?"

"I'd be lying if I said I had a magical solution or that I can foresee where you'll go from here without continued treatment."

A shivering sigh escaped Erron. "At least you've always been honest with me, Doc. I appreciate it."

Dr. Bosch turned off the screen and gave Erron his undivided attention. The clinical detachment of a physician softened before Erron's eyes, and he knew the examination was over.

A fine crease formed across the bridge of Bosch's nose. "You're still going to follow through with your plan?"

"What do you expect? Look at me. I'm useless and that's probably not going to change."

"You don't know that."

"Neither do you."

No, Erron wasn't sure. There was little power in his skill to see his future beyond knowing how hard his life had become. The knowledge pressed into his chest, unseen yet cumbersome. Erron foresaw the stares of people who lived outside of physical ailments. The multitudes who existed without strangeness or medical oddities. He didn't want to be unique if it landed him a role in the local freak show.

"Living with a disability is not the end of the universe, Erron." The doctor placed his hand on Erron's shoulder, clearly to comfort, but the warm contact fractured the tenuous facade holding Erron's composure intact. The invisible weight on his chest deepened, stressing his heart.

"Easy to say when you're not the one living with it." Erron gasped as his eyes misted.

"I can understand your frustration—"

"Am I cleared to leave sick bay, Doctor?" A single tear ran down to Erron's jaw.

Dr. Bosch paused. Sympathy colored his expression, any remnants of his previous energy defused. "Yes. I've already informed the command crew. Would you like an escort to your quarters?"

Erron struggled off the bed, shaking off the doctor's attempt to help. The tattered sheet of his self-esteem was only held together by stubborn threads. It would take more than the deep hissing breath to center himself, but he would make do.

"No. I have to learn how to live with my own crippled ass."

ERRON FUMBLED AROUND his quarters, his left leg dragging. His footsteps were stable enough to walk, but he didn't trust them all the time. Fortunately, there was no one to witness his fall earlier when he had misjudged the position of the desk chair. A half-empty storage crate sat on his bed, piles of clothing next to it. He moved to the open closet and picked out a purple shirt with a row of buttons down the front. The hanger still through the shoulders, Erron reached for the buttons to release it.

He couldn't open the shirt. The buttons were less than a centimeter wide and his fingers weren't capable of closing on them properly. The grip was there, but the fine dexterity for performing minute tasks was still developing. However fucking long it would take.

Snarling, Erron snatched the shirt off the rack, hanger and all, and threw it into the far corner. It crumpled into a worthless pile, and he wondered if he should just join it. So much easier than the current struggles. Jaw clenched, he pondered his future. Were even the simplest things to be beyond him now?

No.

Erron was going to take care of himself. It was what he'd been doing since Toby left and it was what he would do from now on. He just needed to do it somewhere else.

Taking a deep breath, he pulled a few more garments and shambled to the bed. One by one, he loaded the crate with his belongings. He didn't really have much to work with, but his physical limitations were going to make this a long night. The ship was scheduled to land on Alpha Centauri in two days. He needed to be ready by then.

This was the first time he'd been able to return to his room, let alone allowed to move about the ship unescorted since the stroke. Erron longed for a shower. He hadn't bathed properly since this began. However, the prospect of being seen as he tried to wash himself with his ham-handed body gave him pause. He just wasn't ready for that.

As he worked his way back to the closet, the door chime sounded. He stood motionless, a cold wave of nerves gripping him. No one was supposed to be there. Perhaps they'd just go away.

The chime went off again. Erron ignored it, and a sudden pounding on the door startled him.

"Erron! I know you're in there." Gamin's booming shout came clean and clear through the door. "If you don't open up, I'll call Liam and Doc Bosch and have them take you back to sick bay!"

Lacking the desire to be defiant, Erron padded over to the hatch. He tapped the control, trying to forget his shaky hand, and stepped back as the door slid wide.

Gamin stood before him, scruffy and unshaven. He wore his work clothes complete with stained apron and held in one hand a small covered bowl. It was the first time in two weeks Erron had laid eyes on the man, and he nearly whimpered. The sight of Gamin made his chest ache, but he held his ground, refusing to beg for the man's embrace. Too much had gone wrong and would continue to go wrong. Leaving was best for everyone.

"Can I come in?"

Without speaking, Erron gestured and stepped aside. Gamin placed the bowl on the desk and turned back to Erron. Edgy and impatient, he looked over every square centimeter of Erron. After two weeks of being prodded and scanned by Dr. Bosch, he was not happy to be examined yet again. Erron knew wrapping his clumsy arms around himself was a futile attempt to hide. He was fully aware of what he looked like in the mirror. No one else needed to see it.

Desperate to break Gamin's scrutiny, Erron's question was sharper than intended. "What's in the bowl?"

"Your dinner." He pulled the lid off and Erron caught the aroma, enflaming his hunger in an instant. "I know you skipped the last meal service. Sit down and eat. You look exhausted."

Erron glanced at the time stamp on his monitor. It had taken far too long for what little he'd accomplished. As much as it chaffed him, Gamin was right. With Erron's poor endurance, it took nothing to wear him down. He worked his way to the desk, hoping Gamin wasn't watching the sad way he shuffled and said a silent thanks when Gamin didn't pull out the chair and try to seat him.

"Thank you, Gamin. I needed a break."

The stew looked so inviting, and Erron was relieved to find the spoon Gamin brought along had a fat handle. He would have an easier time managing. The thought of Gamin watching him drop the utensil over and over, spilling food on himself, made him cringe. Gamin had obviously thought ahead. The wonderful first spoonfuls told Erron how hungry he really was. Caught up in his meal, Erron allowed himself to forget the rotten events of this year until Gamin surveyed the room.

"Erron? Are you packing?" The disappointment in Gamin's voice was a foul sauce.

Feeling guiltier than when he made the decision, Erron paused for a moment and nodded. He couldn't say it out loud.

"You're leaving? Why?"

Erron set down the spoon and blurted it out. "Because I'm useless, Gamin."

"How can you say that? It's only been two weeks."

"I can't pull my weight here. I can't pick up and use a knife properly. How am I supposed to cook like this?"

"We can adjust. Everyone on board will understand."

"I can't ask everyone else to change for my benefit. I may never be back to what I was before."

"What does that have to do with anything?"

Erron's volume increased along with his frustration. "Everyone's going to make fun of me or feel sorry for me. I'm going to be a burden on the whole crew. How can I stay?"

"I don't care. I don't want you to go." Jaw tight, Gamin crossed his arms over his chest in defiance.

Erron stared up at the most important man in his world, his gaze like a carving knife in its precision. "It's not your choice."

Gamin fidgeted and snarled without sound as he chewed on Erron's response. In the end, he uncrossed his arms and slumped them to his sides. His whole body stood deflated and beaten, one more thing for Erron to be responsible for. Erron's eyes stung. The sight was killing him.

"Maybe I should go. I can't make you stay if you don't want to. You obviously have work to do." Gamin slouched his head down as his voice broke.

Erron stood from the chair and stepped closer. "I'm sorry, Gamin. I should have said something, to you of all people, but this has been hard enough to deal with."

"I don't like it, but"—his voice fractured—"I understand." Gamin held out his arms and enveloped Erron inside them.

Erron's breath left in a rush as Gamin's musky scent filled his nose and his body heat warmed his flesh. This was the contact he'd always sought. It was familiar and exciting and all too intoxicating to do anything but return the affection. It might be the last time they'd ever see one another. The embrace deepened as Gamin placed a soft kiss to the top of Erron's head.

"Tell me one thing." Gamin's voice shook as he spoke. "Was what James said about you and me during the fight in the mess hall true?"

Because he's in love with you, you fat bastard!

Erron hadn't stopped hearing those words repeat in his head since the moment he'd woke in the infirmary. Had he simply been blind to his own feelings? Was this the real reason his relationship with Barrus and James had stalled instead of flourished? Afraid of the truth, he still tipped back his head to find Gamin's eyes. The world halted as Gamin's breath stilled, his intense gaze pleading for an answer. Chewing his lower lip, Erron's brow creased as he nodded silently.

Gamin wasted no time in planting his mouth over Erron's.

This was no fatherly kiss. Greedy and unexpected, it heated at once, flavored by need and plundering his senses with the familiar qualities uniquely Gamin. His large firm hands slid upward into Erron's hair, holding his head in place as if Erron might bolt given the opportunity. As if he would. Every doubt he'd had of what Gamin meant to him burned away with the fierce demand singing through the full lips on his, the forceful tongue licking along his own. A moan filled the room. It shocked Erron to know it was his own. Gamin's beard scrubbed Erron's skin with a ferocious bite as the fevered embrace tightened, but the sensation fluttered somewhere closer to heaven. He floated on euphoric bliss as the kiss softened. Gamin pulled back slowly, his hungry eyes locked on Erron's mouth, the tip of his tongue tracing the lingering taste along his own bottom lip.

"I should have done that a long time ago." Gamin's speech was breathy and heated.

"Why didn't you?"

Gamin's forehead furrowed as he shook his head. "I don't know if I can explain it."

"I know about Niven, Gamin." Shock etched across Gamin's face. "You became so upset when I said his name, and everyone was so secretive. I needed to know who he was. I wanted to know how to help you. I couldn't stand to see you hurting so badly." Erron reached up and caressed the unshaven jawline. "That's why you panicked when we woke up together that night? Because of him?"

"In a way." Gamin's features twisted as he forced out his explanation. "I was dreaming of you, and then I woke up with you under me. In the bed I shared with Niven. No one had been there since he died. It was like I had cheated on my husband. I didn't handle it well. Well…you know. You were there.

"It was bad enough how much I worried when you went to the poker game. I know what those can be like, especially one of Priest's. I felt like it was wrong to be with you, but I didn't want you with anyone else. Does that make sense?"

"Yes. To me it does. Although, loving Niven doesn't mean you never get to be happy again."

Gamin combed his fingers through Erron's hair. "Niven's been gone for over three years. I will never stop missing him, but it doesn't mean I can't love you just as much."

"I wish you'd said something."

"I didn't get the chance. By the time I sorted my head out enough to talk about it, you announced you'd started seeing James and Barrus."

It really was about the timing, wasn't it? Erron didn't regret the time he spent with James and Barrus, except for the breakup, because it gave him the self-confidence to survive the damage Toby had inflicted. What would it have been like if Gamin had had his chance instead? What different chain of events might they have lived? Had the same drama been destined to repeat itself forever but perhaps in different ways? There was no way to be sure, but one factor couldn't be ignored.

"Before I say anything else, I have to say this." Erron took a deep breath to marshal his nerve. "Your drinking scares me, Gamin. I have enough reason to be self-destructive without you doing it around me."

"I know. It's a habit I picked up when Niven died. I'd always been a drinker before, but I was hurting so bad, I learned a whole new level of escapism. After I got back on my feet, I told myself I was fine, but I still have trouble coping with major issues."

Gamin closed his eyes and let out a deep exhale. "When you came on board, it dug up a lot of conflicts for me. I wanted to protect you and I wanted to keep you all for myself. It didn't take long before I needed a drink because I didn't know how to handle the stress. Then I had to watch you with the two of them. It only got worse."

"They treated me well, Gamin."

"I know. That didn't make it any better."

Slowly, he opened his eyes, and Erron saw the bottomless wells of sorrow. Thick with shame, Gamin's words continued to become coarser with every syllable he uttered.

"I tried to tell myself I was fine until I saw how much it bothered you when we were on Datham, especially after you told me about your mother. That's why I stopped a few days before the whole thing in the mess hall. I knew you were trying to say I needed some help. Doc Bosch has me on the addiction-treatment protocol. I was planning to talk to you about it after the dinner service, before everything went to hell. I am so sorry you ever had to take care of me when I was that far under the influence. You should have never had to help me to bed that night."

Can anyone's DNA open anyone else's quarters?

"I don't want you to go, Erron. I want you here. I want you to be my family forever."

Family? That sounded wonderful. Everything Gamin said was everything he'd always wanted to hear. Then why were the doctor's words salting the moment?

The only other way I can think of is if a blood relative keyed open the door.

Erron stiffened and his eyes grew wide as he chanted, "No. No. No. No. No. This is so wrong, Gamin."

"What do you mean?" Gamin gripped tightened as Erron thrashed to get free. His voice rose and he slapped at Gamin's body with his weak hands, his mind racing. He was so close. The universe couldn't be this unfair, could it?

"I can't do this."

"What's going on?"

"Let go of me!"

Gamin gave Erron a shake, breaking his growing hysteria. "Erron, what are you talking about?"

Erron froze, his body quaking as his halting voice gasped out of him. "I think you're my father."

Gamin's hold relaxed, but Erron lost the will to flee once the words were out. Barely whispers, they held such oppressive power. Never had an idea hit Erron with such a physical force. It stole his breath. Gamin stood unmoving, his blank expression telling nothing. He blinked several times, as if unable to accept the information.

"No, Erron. I'm not." Gamin continued to shake his head.

"But my hand opened your door that night. Only a blood relative can do that. The doctor said so." Erron dipped his head down. He couldn't look Gamin in the eye if the man was going to lie to him. "That explains why you left all those years ago. That's what you and Mom argued about, isn't it?"

"Erron. First, I am *not* your father. I *never* touched your mother. Ever. Even with as much partying we did back then, it never happened. I had Liam add your DNA scan to my quarters about a week after we left Alpha Centauri. I trusted you with everything back in the day and I still do. Second, that is not what the argument was about the last time I spoke to your mom."

This disaster was flaring into something hot. "Then you'd better start explaining quick if you expect me to believe you."

Gamin stepped back, gripping Erron's arms, and directed him to sit down on the edge of the bed. Being moved around without a word was not improving Erron's mood. Gamin sat next to him, let out a generous sigh, and began.

"The day your mother and I had our fight, you were about nineteen. You came out of the shower with just a towel wrapped around your waist and I realized you weren't the little boy I watched grow up anymore. You were a grown man." Gamin paused and wet his lips. "A very...attractive grown man.

"Your mother must have noticed me staring a little too long because as soon as you were out of the room, she fucking lit into me. She was beyond pissed off. She accused me of being a pedophile and said I was helping her rear her child until I got my chance to bed you down as soon as you were old enough.

"I got so angry. I said a lot of ugly things too. I told her the reason she kept fucking losers was that she really wanted me, and there wasn't enough alcohol in the cluster to get me to go where so many men had gone before. Those were just the highlights."

Erron winced. "Ouch."

"When I left and began to calm down, I started believing what she said about me and you. Why else would my best friend say something like that to me? They're supposed to know you better than yourself, right? I couldn't face either one of you, so I stayed away. I didn't contact her. She didn't contact me. You guys were my only family, so then I didn't have much of anyone. It was a lonely time in my life. By the time I finally admitted to myself she was wrong—that I was not some child predator—the civil war broke out and everything just drifted."

"Then who is my father?"

Gamin frowned. "Some joker named Larry she met at the pub. I didn't like him from the moment they met, but she refused to listen. As usual. He was a loser, and when he found out she was pregnant, he ran off. It was a two-week fling. She didn't want anything from him other than you, so she never spoke to him again. Last I heard, he died years ago in some freak transport accident. I'm sorry."

Erron leaned forward and rested his head on Gamin's shoulder. "It's okay. Mom told me as much, but I didn't really believe her because I didn't like the story. Looks like she was telling me the truth."

"Yes, she was." Gamin stroked his hand along the small of Erron's back.

"It's not important who he was. You were the closest thing to a father I had back in those days." Erron grimaced. "Let's not talk about where this is going in comparison. It's a little too ancient-Greek tragedy for me right now."

Gamin chuckled. "All right. If it helps, after not seeing you for so long, when you boarded the ship, I stopped thinking of myself as your father-type and more of your daddy-type."

The hard blush in Erron's cheeks set his face on fire. "So what do we do now?"

"First, you eat up. You need your strength." Gamin urged Erron back to the desk and his uneaten meal. "When the ship lands in Alpha Centauri, we're spending our five days in port getting to know each other the way we should have from the point you set foot on board."

Smiling the whole time, he worked his way to the bottom of the bowl, while Gamin unpacked Erron's crate and put everything back. Most items ended up in the wrong place, but Erron wasn't about to complain. The universe was finally in alignment, granting him a positive event in the midst of the strife.

"Finished?" Gamin asked.

Erron nodded.

Gamin rolled back the chair and hoisted Erron upright into his arms. "Do you trust me?"

Erron nodded again.

"Good. Come with me." Gamin released Erron and stepped back, offering him his hand. Accepting it, Erron ignored the suspicion glazing his thoughts. With a careful step, Gamin touched the door control and led them into the hallway.

"Where are we going?" Erron swiveled his head, looking down both directions for passersby.

"Showers."

"What?" A skewer of panic drove itself into Erron's chest.

"We're both in dire need."

Erron dug in his heels. "Wait." Despite being stronger, Gamin stopped at the first resistance.

"What's the matter?"

"I...I..." Images of others, of pointed fingers and hysterical laughter burst through Erron's head. Deep down, he knew it was irrational, but the fear had its claws in him.

"What are you scared of?"

"I'm..." Erron dipped his head toward the floor when he couldn't complete the sentence.

Gamin closed the gap and lifted Erron's head with a gentle coaxing to his chin. "When we first launched and you were terrified to leave Alpha Centauri, I promised to take care of you. Remember?"

"Yes."

"That hasn't changed." Gamin placed a light kiss on Erron's lips. "I'm going to do a better job now that I have you. I want the chance to learn your body so we can make the most of our shore leave. Come with me. Please."

Erron shuddered at the concept. The idea of being cared for by Gamin pushed back the haunting thoughts. Not erasing them, but shunting their screams out of the forefront. Gamin didn't ask again, only stood waiting as he dropped another patient kiss on Erron's lips. Trust was something Erron held for Gamin as long as his memory existed. There was no reason to divert from their history.

"Okay."

The walk to the lockers and showers was short, but Erron still winced at every sound, afraid of running into a crew member who might stop and gawk. Gamin took his time, letting Erron's slow gait set the pace. The lack of onlookers comforted him as Gamin selected a locker near the shower entrance. Gamin kicked off his shoes and untied his dirty apron, then dropped it on the nearby bench.

The sounds of running water renewed Erron's anxious pulse. They weren't alone. The fear threatened to resurface until Erron recognized what was happening in front of him. With a slow move, Gamin gathered the edge of his shirt, lifted it, and peeled it off, centimeter by centimeter. They'd been in the showers at the same time before, but this was different. Gamin's smoldering eyes never wavered away from Erron. It was a show for his benefit.

And Erron liked the show.

A pair of swollen nipples begged to be suckled, peeking out from the salt-and-pepper whorls of hair shaping Gamin's wide chest. Mesmerized, Erron followed the line of fur covering the swell of his firm belly. Gamin snapped open his pants, teasing at a hint of what lay hidden beneath the mound of his fly. He slid his hands into the waistline and skimmed the clothing down over his thick thighs. The sight of the meaty appendage flopping free made Erron gasp. Stepping out of his pants, Gamin stood tall before Erron in his full majesty.

Broad and strong, Gamin lacked the primping and finishing of a fitness fanatic. No tiny waist. No hard crevices defining each individual muscle and sinew. It didn't matter. Big and barrel-chested, to Erron, Gamin was pure masculinity, solid and all man. Flawless.

The glorious trance broke when Gamin reached for the edge of Erron's shirt. Frozen in terror, he did nothing as Gamin lifted his shirt up and over his head. Gamin kneeled down and unzipped Erron's pants, then drew the garment and his underwear down to his ankles, not stopping until Erron was stripped bare.

This was the moment Erron dreaded. Gamin stood upright, his gaze roaming over every square millimeter of Erron's exposed body. He knew his shoulders no longer sat level, his left side weaker than the right. The lilting stance, and the curl in his limbs, made him asymmetrical in a way Erron could barely stand to look at. How could Gamin?

"You're so beautiful."

Erron frowned with doubt. "How can you say that? I'm not what I was."

"You're still the same man inside. That's what I see. It's always been about wanting *you*."

The intensity in Gamin's confession spoke volumes of truth. There was nothing held back, free for perhaps the first time to voice his needs. And the need was audible. Gamin didn't seem to care about the frailty of Erron's body. He didn't shrink away at the sight. It didn't diminish the heat in his stare. Gamin wanted Erron and the reality held him dumbfounded. Only the sound of wet feet slapping on the tile broke the moment.

"Evening, Liam," Gamin said.

Dripping wet and scrubbing a towel over the tight crop of his auburn hair, Liam entered the locker area. The sergeant was enormous, every bulging muscle on full display. Erron kept his head up high even as a new wave of nerves simmered. For the first time ever in his life, it seemed wrong to look at another man's cock.

"Hey, Gamin." Liam glanced between the two of them. "It's really good to see you up and about, Erron."

"Thanks, Liam."

"How are you two doing?" Liam stepped over to a nearby locker and dried himself without a hint of modesty, brushing the towel over every hill and valley.

"We're doing very well. It looks like I've managed to convince Erron to stay with us."

"That's great! I wasn't thrilled to hear you were going to leave."

Erron tried not to stare as Liam slipped a pair of shorts over his round haunches. "Gamin is very persuasive."

"I'd like to take care of my boy, Liam. If it's not too much to ask under the circumstances, we could use a little privacy."

At the words "my boy," Liam paused and scanned over the two men. A pleasant, nonjudgmental smile brightened his face. "Consider it done."

Reaching into his pocket, Liam placed a pair of tech in his ears. Tapping its edge, the muffled sounds of music hummed into the room.

Liam spoke far too loud over the noise in his ears. "Take as long as you need."

Collecting spare towels from the supply closet, Gamin led Erron into the showers, hanging them on hooks to the right of the entrance. Liam took his place in the doorway, giving his back to the tiled room. A human wall, no one was getting past the hulking sergeant. He stared ahead into the locker room, and with the volume raised, it was doubtful he could hear anything.

If Gamin noticed the lurch in Erron's step, he didn't say a word as he guided them to a station at the far end of the room, with a light touch at Erron's waist. After starting the water, Gamin positioned Erron in the spray and wet his head and back. Erron gave into Gamin, allowing him to soak his hair. Gamin gathered a handful of soap and massaged his firm hands into Erron's scalp, the lather building into lazy streams of foam. It was hard to keep his eyes open, but he didn't want to miss a moment.

After rinsing Erron clean, Gamin began a new exploration with suds, washing every ounce of flesh within his reach. He paid close attention to everything, giving equal time to Erron's fingers as well as the small of his back. Each unhurried contact and stroke of Gamin's hands cleansed away the last of Erron's doubts. The race of his heart lacked the earlier terror. Want screamed along the edge of Erron's skin in a way Toby, James, or Barrus never created.

This was right.

Two weeks of sick-bay seclusion under constant monitoring held Erron's desire in check, assuming he had any as he recovered. Gamin's caresses brought his libido to life, and given the heated organ jutting against him, the chef was no better off. Turgid and purple, the fat head wept a slippery trail on Erron's hip, not a product of soap or water. Entranced by its swollen beauty, he reached after it, only to have Gamin snatch his wrist.

"Not yet. No one's touched me since Niven. My trigger's already half pulled."

Erron's brow rose in disbelief. "You haven't been with anyone since Niven?"

"I've had a few offers, but I turned them down."

"What were you waiting for?"

Gamin's voice broke as it dropped to a whisper. "Someone worth it."

Erron looped his arm over Gamin's shoulder and pulled himself up to capture Gamin's mouth. The kiss was messy and urgent. Growling, Gamin returned the fervor, cupping Erron's ass, dipping his fingers into the cleft. Erron moaned like a wanton whore when Gamin circled his aching cock with his other hand.

"You're mine," Gamin snarled against Erron's mouth. "You feel so good in my hands. Gonna make you come so hard, boy."

Erron writhed as every one of his senses urged him on. "Oh, Gamin, fuck yes."

Cautious and tender was gone, replaced by furious strokes slick with suds and arousal. Gamin's fingers dug into Erron's tender opening as the shower pelted his overheated flesh. There wasn't much left of his stamina. The pot was boiling over. Gamin slammed his mouth over Erron's and swallowed the growing howl as his grasp firmed. Erron reached between them and captured Gamin's unwavering penis. Three more frantic strokes and both men screamed into each other as they burst, streaks of molten pleasure icing their hands and bodies as they stroked and thrust through the endless wave.

They shared gasps and biting kisses as they extended the cooldown as long as possible. Erron was exhausted. When their kiss ended, he dropped his head to Gamin's shoulder. Tremors shook the otherwise steady chef.

"Holy shit." Erron had never come so hard in his life.

Laughing, Gamin brushed his lips along Erron's temple, squeezing him tighter.

They shared another long kiss, this time easy and promising a happy future. Once it gradually ended, Gamin held Erron tight, foreheads touching as the water continued to spray over them. The joy in his eyes sparkled.

"I love you, Erron." Gamin's voice was tight, as if he held a tight rein on his emotions and the grip was tenuous. "I plan on using the rest of my life to make you happy. No matter what."

Erron's eyes watered. "I don't think you'll need that much time."

Chapter Eleven

THEY WERE SUPPOSED to be packing to leave. But somehow, that wasn't what they were doing.

The heavy blue-and-gray comforter twisted in Erron's hands, and he let out another loud moan. Sprawled on his back over the edge of the hotel bed, his shirt sat hiked up to his chest and his pants tangled around his ankles. Erron tried to sit upright, but the weight of Gamin's arms crossing his thighs and his outstretched hand at Erron's chest kept him from rising. Gamin obviously didn't want anything to interrupt his work.

Erron raised his head enough to watch the thick length of his cock disappear into Gamin's greedy mouth. He'd choked a few times the first time he tried when they arrived at the hotel, but the man had been determined and persevered. Once he bottomed out, nose pressed into Erron's groin, he pulled back slow. Gamin's cheeks hollowed in suction as his tongue laved Erron's organ, making his eyes roll back in his head.

The last five days of shore leave had been fantastic. Since Erron had been insecure about the crew seeing him, they'd waited until everyone else had left before disembarking. Tucked in close, they had toured the port with Gamin holding his hand as they walked along at Erron's reduced speed. Hardly anyone had given either man a second look. Erron's shuffling feet and uneasy movements drew no fascination from the crowds. No laughter. No pitying looks and pointed fingers. Nothing. Everyone surrounding them had appeared to have their own business to attend, and the lack of attention made Erron forget about the visible remnants of his condition.

After finishing the special purchasing for the ship, Erron and Gamin had spent the rest of the time sampling restaurants and exploring each other in the hotel room. Gamin acted insatiable and starved for physical contact. Erron was not complaining.

Erron's back arched as Gamin continued to swallow his turgid flesh, tip to root, over and over again. Another audible spike of pleasure escaped him over Gamin's enthusiastic feeding. The bed had been freshly made not ten minutes before, but it was a shambles now as Erron used it to give voice to the sensations he couldn't express properly. He was fast losing himself to Gamin's ministrations.

The sloppy, needy sounds of suckling were too much. Erron pressed his head back into the bed as he lost the fight to prolong the ecstasy muddling his mind. The surges ran in lightning strikes from his extremities and converged on his groin. An uncontrolled wail filled the room as Erron unleashed into Gamin's waiting mouth. The orgasmic tremors hadn't even settled before Gamin growled and flipped him over onto his stomach.

Still mewling into the sheets, Erron felt the halves of his backside pried apart to immediately be assaulted by Gamin's mouth and tongue. Every sensation of licking and chewing centered on his opening. An unusual amount of liquid heat pooled in the sensitive ring. Erron shivered as he realized Gamin hadn't swallowed. It wasn't the first time he'd continued their play using Erron's semen. From the frenzy of Gamin's grunts and intensity, there wouldn't be an extended preamble before he claimed his prize. Fortunately, Erron had many rehearsals over the last five days.

With a lusty chuckle, Gamin clambered up Erron's prone body, placing the blunt heat of his cock against the tender opening begging to give way. A needy sigh escaped Erron as Gamin's weight settled over him and breached him at the same time. Erron had gained a great deal of practice accepting the fat stalk. Once he bottomed out, Gamin wasted no time getting things started.

Gamin's lust was somewhere short of unrestrained yet not exactly gentle. From this position, each thrust ground Erron's cock into the bed and battered that sweet spot inside him. He had yet to soften and the dual action was fast building a second charge. The possibility of another orgasm was there.

Erron pleaded, lost and delirious. "Gamin... Don't stop... Please...."

The blinding rush swept through Erron faster than he acknowledged it. The spontaneity, the delicious weight of Gamin's body, and the perfect internal stroke shattered him again. A strangled cry burst out of him, coming in staccato bursts matching Gamin's pounding. His body's spasms tightened around the rigid piece of meat inside him.

"I can't... You're squeezing me so good..." Gamin's words turned into a series of snarling noises as he flooded Erron's insides. Trickles of wet heat spilled out of Erron as Gamin continued to pant and thrust until his movements slowed to something less erratic.

When Gamin finally softened and slipped out, the pair shared an exhausted fit of laughter.

"I wasn't exactly expecting that." Erron's smile risked becoming permanent.

Gamin brushed a kiss along Erron's temple. "I couldn't resist. You just looked good enough to eat." Gamin's weight shifted as he glanced to the timepiece on the dresser. "Oh shit! We have to get out of here before our check-in expires!"

The bed bounced as Gamin leaped up and rushed to the bathroom. He returned with a wet cloth to quickly clean the tacky mess from Erron, but the bed covers were beyond hope at this point. Gamin rushed to help Erron up and put his clothes back together in some semblance of decency. It was a mad race to throw everything they brought along into their soft cylinder-shaped bag before hurrying out the door.

As they made their way through the hallway to the main desk, Erron looked back at their room. He was going to miss the lovely sanctuary the hotel had been for the last five days.

"I feel a little guilty for the condition we left the room in." Erron shuffled along as best he could. Gamin was being patient, but there was no question he was itching to go faster.

"Can't be helped. I'm not paying for another day here if we can't make good use of it. We're taking off this evening."

"I know. But, fuck me, they'll know what we were up to before we left." A blush crept into Erron's cheeks. "Our DNA is all over the bed."

Gamin giggled and shrugged. "And the shower. And the writing desk. And the carpet. And the sitting-room chair. What's your point?"

"Ugh. When you put it that way, I guess I don't have one." Erron snickered. "Who knew you had that much energy?"

A burst of laughter spilled out of Gamin as they reached the front desk. They checked out with time to spare, which gave Erron great pleasure. The last thing he wanted was his infirmities to be a problem. The main doors slid open and Gamin flagged a transport to take them back into the main density of the spaceport. Settling into the back seat, Gamin keyed in the destination as Erron slumped against Gamin's sturdy frame.

"Hungry?"

Erron couldn't stifle the erupting yawn. "Yeah, but I'm burnt toast. I wasn't prepped to come twice."

"We'll take a nap before we get some food." Gamin leaned over and kissed the top of Erron's head.

"But we already checked out."

"That's okay. I have an idea." Gamin reached forward and keyed a new destination. The vehicle turned at the next junction and headed for the center of the port.

When the transport stopped, Erron stepped out and found himself in the port's arboretum. In the middle of the chaotic throng of travelers and merchants sat this perfect little section of utopia. Large gardens divided by real cobblestone paths drew inexorable lines directly to the elaborate water fountain at its center. The soft rush of water combined with the actual breeze created by the gargantuan skylight above them was like stepping through a fantasy mirror into a world that didn't rely on technology and architecture to define it, but rather nature and beauty.

Gamin led Erron to one of the many long benches found along the walking paths and dropped their bag on one end. "Let's take a nap, then we can get some food." Lying down on his back he used their luggage as a pillow. "We have at least four hours to burn before we need to be back on board."

"Here?" Erron peered around at the various people sharing the park. The sheer number quickened his heartbeat and made his breath into a series of short huffs. "Aren't you worried about what these people think?"

Gamin reached out to take Erron's hand, urging him to lie on top of his prone body. "Nope. We launch in about eight hours. We'll probably never see any of these people again in our lifetimes. Why should I care as long as I have my boy in my arms?"

Erron settled on top of Gamin, luxuriating in how decadently comfortable the man under him was. Big and powerful with just enough padding. Gamin wrapped his arms around him, ending any thoughts Erron had of falling to the ground below. The warmth radiating off Gamin soaked into Erron's skin and lulled him into a drowsy state. Peeking around the scattered travelers, Erron found no one caring what they were doing. Everyone went on their own path, oblivious to anyone outside their vision, including him and Gamin.

The only frustrating aspect of their vacation was Erron's stamina. He tired easily, but even Dr. Bosch said the condition was normal under the circumstances and would ultimately pass. So Gamin had made sure to feed him up, sex him up, and take plenty of nap time, which often led to more sex over the last five days.

Erron was able to walk, more or less. He limped a bit with his slow left foot but managed if he was careful. His hands sometimes refused to obey him and the fine-tuning of his grip was restricted. Handling a minute item like a standard eating utensil brought him endless grief, but thicker items, like Gamin's dick, he worked just fine. That, and the fact his sex drive and functions were intact, made up for a lot of the other things.

"Are you sure we're doing the right thing?" Erron's voice was weary as he rested, riding the rise and fall of Gamin's chest.

"What do you mean?"

"Me going back to work on the *Santa Claus*. Do you think it will be all right?"

Gamin stroked Erron's scalp with his fingertips. "You're going to be fine. You're just nervous. Doc Bosch gave you the all clear. And I don't want you away from me. When you went down in the mess hall and then the two weeks you refused to see anyone, those were the scariest days of my life. It was like I was losing my last chance to be with you. I need you with me, Erron. Forever."

"I need you too." Erron sighed with a grin. "Thank you for this getaway. It's making me think less about what I lost when the stroke hit and more about how far I've come since it happened."

"You almost died."

Erron nodded against the warm chest under him. "I know. Do you think the rest of the crew will look at me funny?"

"No. They're just happy to see you alive and well. I've gotten a lot of coms from them while we've been gone here."

"Really?"

"Just good wishes and messages hoping you're coming back. You made a good impression on everyone, Erron. I'd hate to disappoint them after all of this."

Erron yawned, his words barely audible. "Me too."

The bubbling of the fountain behind them gently tickled the recesses of Erron's consciousness while the body heat radiating from underneath softened him like molten caramel. Adding in the massaging strokes of Gamin's touch, and Erron drifted away, content on the perfect human mattress beneath him. In the fresh air, surrounded by the subtle fragrance of fresh trees, flowers, and Gamin's scent, he never slept so well.

"ARE WE THE first ones back on board?"

Gamin gave Erron a curious glance. "Why do you ask?"

Erron stared down the empty hallway. "Because we launch in three hours, we're on Beta deck where everyone lives, and we've yet to set eyes on anyone."

The large hand surrounding Erron's was a surrogate lifeline as he and Gamin walked down the quiet corridor. Erron was anxious enough about finally seeing the crew after his stroke. Their absence was not improving his nerves. Would they accept his limitations now? Would they find him a burden on the ship? Plenty of time was spent by Gamin reassuring him, but now with the time here, those little nagging thoughts were gaining volume.

Erron squeezed Gamin's hand tighter. Turning his head, Gamin gave him one of those magical, warming smiles of his. A soft, bass-filled chuckle tickled Erron's nerves.

"They're not hiding from you if that's what you're worried about."

Erron scowled. "Don't make fun of me."

"Never, my dear." Gamin bent down and kissed Erron's hand linked to his own. "The others are probably just taking their time getting back. We don't usually have this many days in port in one stretch."

Frowning while giving Gamin a dirty glare, Erron accepted the explanation, but it didn't calm his agitation. He struggled to make extra sure he wasn't dragging his left foot too much in case they ran into someone. Gamin had become used to his current walking rhythm, with its staggered limp. It was exhausting to hide, and he wasn't sure how successful the effort was, but he didn't want to accentuate it for others to see when the time came.

"Come on, Erron. Let's go down to the kitchen and make sure the new cooking gear actually showed up."

Erron rolled his eyes, thinking of the worst scenario. "Oh, please. The last thing I need right now is to have to wait for that order to come back around on our next port here." Speeding his pace, he pulled Gamin along on the way to the lift.

"In a hurry?" Gamin snickered.

In a way, yes, he was. A lot of work went into the kitchen's special purchases on this trip and they were critical as far as Erron was concerned. Keeping up with the crew and the ability to perform his job were entwined with the order. He wasn't sure how he'd handle it, if the delivery was buggered.

Erron surprised himself how fast he came out of the lift when the doors opened. Okay, it wasn't the most graceful exit, but it was quicker than expected. He was so determined to get to the mess hall, he wasn't even holding Gamin's hand for support. He huffed in utter annoyance when he saw the lights were out in the room. It was totally black from the hallway. Even the emergency lamps were down.

"Mrs. Claus, turn on the lights in the mess hall." Erron squinted into the dark as he made it through the doorway.

"Surprise!"

Erron's heart nearly stopped at the sound of the entire crew shouting as the lights came up. Startled, he scrambled backward only to be stopped by the familiar bulk of Gamin. Heart pounding and eyes wide, his gaze skittered around the room.

Everyone was here. The captain, Liam and Hadrian, Dr. Bosch and Carson, and every other crewman filled the room, cheering at him. A banner hung over the buffet counter that read "Welcome Home, Erron!" in giant green and purple text.

Gamin's arms tightened around Erron as his bass-toned whispers drifted across his ear, "And you were worried about them?"

The group filtered forward, each man taking his turn to shake Erron's hand or pass along their well wishes. No pity. No condescension—just honest interest in his well-being and new relationship. Erron was stunned. Unsure of how to act, he did the only natural thing to do. He settled into the warm arms surrounding him with pride and smiled ear to ear.

"Good to have you back, Erron." Captain Danverse clasped Erron's hand. "I hate to have to go through another interview when I have perfectly good staff on hand." Mac stood right beside the captain, young and stocky, he always appeared dirty from doing ship maintenance. In fact, there was a fresh smudge on his cheek.

"Your new tech is installed. I'll give you the tutorial after we settle in after launch." Mac's eyes brightened at the mere mention of new equipment.

"Already? That's incredible!" Erron gushed, he was so excited.

Mac blushed slightly. "It's no big deal. It was easy. But you're gonna love it."

The room grew louder with the multiple voices chatting as the festivities began. The energy between everyone was high as multiple layers of conversation shared the tales of their vacations and adventures over the last five days. Dr. Bosch worked his way to the pair, a genuine grin on his handsome face.

"So did you read my com about the DNA comparison between you two? I made it really short to encourage you to read it."

Erron felt a twinge of embarrassment. When Gamin told him why his DNA opened his quarters, Erron believed him. But Gamin had insisted on messaging the doctor to prove it so there was no doubt. Dr. Bosch's report said there was no possibility Gamin was Erron's father. They were genetically incompatible.

"Yes, I did read it." Erron looked away as he dipped his chin. The smile on his face proved a lack of wounded pride. "I'm sorry. Gamin refused to drop the subject when I told him you said a blood relative's DNA could fool the scanner."

"I also said we didn't have any on board. I run those kinds of comparisons of every crew member. It's just part of my basic write-up. I try to be very thorough." Without missing a beat, Bosch's teasing shifted and his manner bore the professionalism marking him as the ship's head medical officer. "Speaking of which, I expect you in sick bay for a follow-up tomorrow between breakfast and lunch services. I've left my schedule open for you."

Gamin gave Dr. Bosch a quick salute. "I'll make sure he's there, Doc."

"And I intend to continue your physical exercises." Hadrian's sweet accent graced the group with Liam in close tow. "I have been discussing the process with the doctor and he has helped me plan a strategy for you."

Dr. Bosch added his part. "It won't be easy, Erron, but the repetition and strengthening will help increase your stamina and re-educate your body now that you're well stabilized."

"I'm glad to see you decided to stay, Erron." Liam clapping a friendly hand on Erron's shoulder. "It's been a long time since we've seen Gamin smile this much. You must be good for him."

Gamin snugged his arms tight for a moment before dropping a kiss on top of Erron's head. "The best thing ever, Liam."

Erron stood there chatting back and forth with the crew as the party continued. Gamin stayed wrapped around him the entire time. At first he thought it was some kind of territorial display for the crew, but he realized Gamin held him upright, and kept him from having to move around as much. Gamin was trying to make things easier for him. As Gamin repeated multiple times through their shore leave, he wanted Erron to be happy. And Erron was.

The mood was high, but something was missing. James and Barrus had yet to be seen amongst the crowd. It wasn't that he should be surprised, but their absence tainted the occasion. Erron sighed. It was a bit much to expect them to appear under the circumstances.

"All right, you mangy lot! Food is served!" Came the shout through the hall.

Erron twisted around until he faced Gamin. "Food? Who the hell did you actually let in our kitchen?"

"Take a look." Gamin nodded in the direction of the buffet-service line.

Through the kitchen doors, James and Barrus came bearing steaming food trays. Their aprons were stained as broadly as the grins shining on their faces. Dropping the last of the serving pans into place, they checked the warmers and stepped away from the counter.

James shouted to the crowd. "You guys can serve yourselves. This was fun, but in the future, we'll be leaving this to the professionals." He caught Erron's eye and gave him a wink. James and Barrus both removed their aprons and headed in Erron's direction.

Patting Gamin's arms, Erron turned to catch his eyes with a silent, pleading request. Gamin nodded in return, no words needed. He released Erron with an approving grin.

No longer caring about his limp, Erron closed the gap between the three and threw himself into their arms. James and Barrus held him tight, a tight rush flooding Erron's chest. With every touch, came a sense of relief, true love without lust. They brushed back Erron's hair, and touched his face and shoulders, examining him without the medical curiosity he endured for the two weeks after the stroke. No one said a word for a long time as they held their silent absolutions for each other.

"We missed you so much, Erron. We almost died when Carson called out the medical emergency. We're so sorry you thought you couldn't face us afterward." James's eyes were glossy yet elated. Erron swallowed hard to fight back the overflow of feelings that mirrored the happiness of all three men. They were moments away from a cascade of teary eyes.

Barrus kissed Erron's forehead. "And for the way we acted before it imploded."

"You had your reasons."

"That doesn't make it right."

Erron shook his head. "It's not important. It was just a bad day all over."

"We still want to be your good friends, Erron."

"I'd like that."

A pair of large, warm hands gently squeezed Erron's shoulders. He pivoted his head to find Gamin behind him, supporting him as usual.

"We'd both like that."

Erron beamed at Gamin's approval and he raised his hands, covering Gamin's with his own.

Barrus reached out and pulled James closer. "Thanks for letting us do this, Gamin."

"And helping us pull it off." James leaned into Barrus's side.

Erron turned, looking at each man in turn. "You three are responsible for this?"

"Yep. We know our way around a kitchen, but with you two on board, we don't need to do it very often." Barrus shrugged. "After we were let off our confinement to quarters, we had a chance to talk. Liam got the three of us together to work it out because he was tired of running messages back and forth about your condition."

"We realized that we had your best interests at heart, and had to admit that Gamin was in your best interest." James smiled as he pushed a lock of hair behind Erron's ear. "We wouldn't have made you happy, Erron. You deserve to be with someone you can love back the way you deserve."

Barrus grinned. "You two look really good together."

Everyone seemed a little misty eyed as Gamin clasped a thankful hand on Barrus's shoulder. No one spoke. No doubt everyone feared the amount of emotion likely to spill out if much more was said. Erron was easily at the point of boil-over.

James broke the silence. "How are you doing, Erron? Really."

Erron paused to contemplate that answer. "Better than I should be, to be honest. My body still doesn't do everything it's told, and I'll probably limp for a long time, if not forever. I was scared to see everyone. Terrified, really. I can't believe I'm having a good time tonight."

Gamin kissed his temple. "You deserve it."

"I'm not saying I won't have bad days where I scream and bitch and break things. But I think being on board is a safe place for me to get back to some kind of normal."

"Well, you know we'll help out if you need anything. Just ask," Barrus said.

"And if we get too pushy or too helpful, just tell us to fuck off," James added with a laugh.

Erron snorted. "I don't think you'll have to worry. My speech is fine now."

Gamin pulled Erron back against his chest as his hands rested on the smaller man's waist. Another gentle kiss fluttered against the back of Erron's head, sending a comfy sensation down his spine. It made him press deeper into the embrace.

"It's good to be home."

ERRON DROPPED THE last cucumber into the automatic slicer. With the touch of a single button, the device came to life and a second later, he pulled the bin out filled with perfect 0.3-centimeter-thick slices for the salad. Even though he always loved to do the prep work completely by hand, he entertained himself every time he used the gadget. It had so many different options and uses Erron was ecstatic they had purchased it for the kitchen.

Who needs to know how to use a knife?

Pouring the slices into the large mixing bowl with the rest of ingredients, he tossed the salad using a pair of tongs with extra-wide handles. Erron still had to be careful, but the new utensils and equipment they purchased while on leave made his job much more manageable. Utensils, pans, bowls, and other basic items had been retrofitted or replaced with kitchenware sporting oversized handles to compensate for Erron's grip. A few automated devices were added to take some of the difficulty out of his limitations and make the galley more efficient for both men.

A timer chimed, so Erron set down the salad and shuffled over to the oven. Peering through the window, six large deep trays of Erron's signature lasagna bubbled away in harmony. The crew had been requesting the meal since the welcome party before launch. Since he had what he needed, he didn't see any reason to deny them.

Erron opened the oven door, and the escaping heat dragged an enticing blend of scents with it into the air. The kitchen was alive with the tantalizing aromas. Erron smelled the cheese, meat, and spices balanced so precisely, he didn't need to taste the lasagna to know it was flawless.

"Need any help with that?" Gamin twisted dough into breadsticks, preparing to pop them into the oven once the main dishes were out.

Erron shook his head. "No thanks, I'm good." He slipped on the pair of heat-proof mittens hanging from the utility belt slung around his waist. It held his favorite spoons and spices, those he needed at the ready and had many customizable holsters to adapt as needed. Another special purchase from the last port.

Reaching in, Erron pulled the first full pan from the oven by its oversized handles. Carefully, he sidestepped to the counter and placed the heavy entree on the rack to cook and make itself happy. All the while, Gamin kept an eye on Erron but maintained a respectful distance while he worked. Gamin was good at allowing Erron to test his limits. He was there if Erron needed it but gave him the space he needed to feel as close to normal as possible.

Some of the other crew members weren't as lucky.

They meant well, of course, but a few of them were a little too quick to help, not allowing Erron to do simple tasks he was capable of completing unassisted. It was definitely a hot spot for him. Feeling inadequate was not something he took lightly, as poor Priest found out the hard way.

Erron apologized for the public scolding he gave the pilot, but afterward the word quickly spread. Now everyone kept their distance and gave him the chance to need help before rushing in like he was some crippled freak in distress. Erron was not a freak or a cripple. It was best if everyone remembered that.

As the last tray made it to the counter, Erron glanced over at Gamin. He was seasoning several trays of uncooked breadsticks while keeping watch from the corner of his eye, never once leaping up from his station. Gamin had never once treated him as disabled. He had let Erron drop a few things and make some mistakes but always waited for Erron to ask for aid.

Erron smiled as he took off his gloves. A warmth filled his chest that had nothing to do with the open oven door. He thought about how it started, the fake gypsy woman and her prediction.

You think you've lost the ability to love another but you'll find it on board once again.

Being right didn't make her any less of a charlatan. Toby had done crippling damage Erron was sure would never heal. But he'd managed to come out from under the rubble with permanent scars and infirmities, somehow better off than when he started.

Erron shuffled over to Gamin before he rose up to place his trays in the now-empty oven. Sliding his arms around the big man's shoulders, he leaned forward and said the one thing into Gamin's ear, after the pain he'd endured, he'd never managed to say aloud.

"I love you, Gamin."

Gamin pivoted around on his stool, still in Erron's embrace. His smile broadened with every second it lay on his face, as his eyes misted. Reaching up, he cupped Erron's face with his large hands and placed a kiss on Erron that nearly made him lose his footing.

"I love you so much, Erron." The searing tone in Gamin's words, Erron recognized. He heard it daily, whenever he was about to be ravaged. His mind began the countdown to a new incident of sexual harassment in the workplace.

Erron whispered in silky tones. "Simmer down, sir. We have a meal to finish and serve. Besides, from what I've heard, I'd think you'd been caught in enough compromising positions on this ship for one lifetime. I know it's been a few years since it's happened, but I'm sure you can recall a few embarrassing moments in your past."

Gamin chuckled even though the heat hadn't left his eyes. Now that everything was out in the open, Niven was no longer an out of bounds subject, even if they didn't talk about him much out of respect.

"About that," Gamin growled as he touched his forehead to Erron's. "Niven wasn't the one with the taste for public sex." He dipped down and placed several gentle bites down Erron's neck and shoulder. "That was all me."

Erron's head rolled back as Gamin pulled him closer. With a twist of his hips, he ground Erron against his growing erection. How the man went to aroused and out of control from nothing, never ceased to amaze Erron. Even if he wasn't really complaining. He ran his hands over the velvety tight crop of Gamin's hair, relishing the feverish suction at the junction of his neck and shoulder.

"This is such an amazing life," Erron gasped as Gamin pushed the trays aside and laid Erron on the counter.

Acknowledgements

A special heartfelt thanks to NineStar Press for giving this book & series new life. I love the care it's received in this new edition.

Thank you members, friends, & staff at Gay Authors.org. Without you all, I might never have had the courage to take this ride.

And a special thanks and love for Tom, who may not have understood my muses (yes, plural) and creative needs, but put up with me and them anyway.

About the Author

While spending years more focused on visual arts, J. Alan Veerkamp never let go of his innate passion for storytelling, wanting to write and draw comic books when he grew up. Once he discovered M/M fiction, a whole new world opened filled with possibilities. Why couldn't you have fantastic and dynamic sexy tales with an M/M cast? He started reading the online tales of authors like, Night Tempest, Rob Colton, and Alicia Nordwell, which only fueled his need to create. Eventually he found GayAuthors.org, and with a little coercive nudge, started sharing his tales with an unexpected level of positive response. The experience and support gave him the courage to cross his fingers and aim for the world of M/M publishing.

Born and raised in Michigan, J. Alan continues to type away, wishing it was practical to use a noisy, old fashioned keyboard that clacks with each strike, if just to annoy his loving partner and spoiled miniature dachshund.

Facebook: www.facebook.com/jalanveerkamp

Twitter: @jalanveerkamp

Website: www.jalanveerkamp.wordpress.com

Other books by this author

The Luxorian Fugitive

Also Available from NineStar Press

Connect with NineStar Press

Website: NineStarPress.com

Facebook: NineStarPress

Facebook Reader Group: NineStarNiche

Twitter: @ninestarpress

Tumblr: NineStarPress